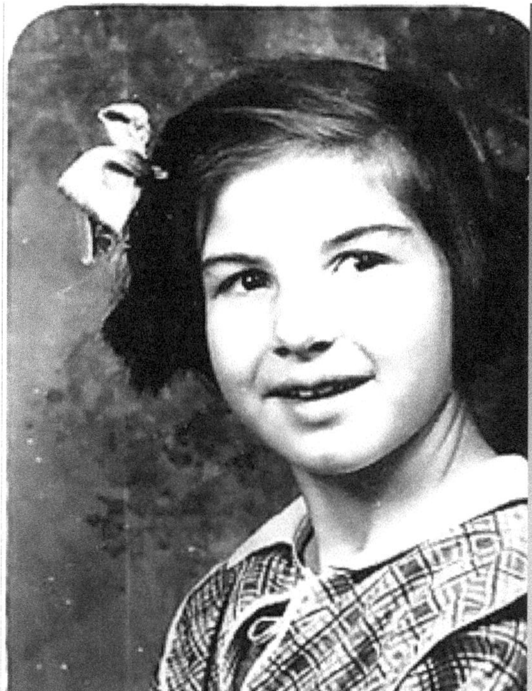

THE SCRAP BOOK OF BURNT OFFERINGS

By

Linda L. Roberts

This book is based on a true story, the letters are original. Surviving a fire is what was found inside the Scrap Book many years later. During WWII a young girl, Betty Lou Ross from a small logging town New Meadows in West Central Idaho, made an effort to make a difference during this turbulent time in our history. The story of what one little girl accomplished to touch so many people.

BURNT OFFERINGS

BETTY LOU ROSS-HUNT

Linda L. Roberts

Acknowledgment

This book is based on a true story, the letters and pictures are original from WWII. A young girl named Betty Lou Ross who tried to help during this turbulent time in our history. What one little girl can accomplish is to touch so many. Betty and her family made their home in Central Idaho. First and foremost I want to thank my Mother Betty Lou Hunt for her dedication, and this treasure.

I also want to thank my family. Without their support I would not have continued with this endeavor to tell the fabulous story of my mother's accomplishments and efforts to help boost the spirits of the troops during WWII.

Sister Suzie, Lindsey, and Lionel Burcham. Brother Kenneth, Carol, Amy, and Teresa Trueba.

Sister cousins Mary Jane Moore, Connie Belnap, Linda Miller. Sisters in-law Becky Papadopoulos, Kerry Coward, Cindy Laws, Netty Hooks, and brother-in-law Rick Shultsmeier, and mother in-law Dixie Roberts Countless precious cousins, spread across the country.

Betty Lou Ross - Hunt is my mother and over the years she has shared many stories of her life and the adventures her and her family have undertaken. She shared with me the story of the scrap book and her letters from the war department, but I had never seen the scrap books she sent. Bettys mother Alma Lea Ross started this adventure that she continued. After mom passed away in 2004 I was going through her belongings and ran across the scrap book she had salvaged from a fire. This is a scrap book she made of the correspondence she got from the scrap books she had sent to the troops.

 My wish is to share this treasure with you and some of the stories I have heard over the years; and the life of her family, including pictures, some of which are of her brothers and in-laws that also served in the war. Many if not most of the people involved in her life have since passed and I cannot discuss details with any of them.

About the Author

Daughter of Betty Lou Ross-Hunt and Floyd E. Hunt, born Oct. 1956 in Council, Idaho. My upbringing was in a logging family in New Meadows, and I currently reside in Meridian, Idaho. My family includes husband Dave Roberts, we've been together 40 years. Son Timothy, and my two adorable grandchildren, River (4 years old) and Quinn (2 years old). Their mother Samee.

My heart belongs to my family, the mountains of Idaho, as I have a deep love for activities such as fishing, hiking, and hunting, which I enjoyed while growing up.

Preface

This book is dedicated to all the men and women that served our great Country on and off the battle field, abroad or here at home during WWII

Names of persons that wrote letters are contained in this scrap book, and relatives that served:

Italy, South Pacific, Coast of Africa

PFC Franklin E. Ross

Corp. Guy W. Ross

Jack Edwin Ross

Marion Howard Conner

Fredrick Ross

Warren Loomis

R. W. Bliss Brigadier General Assistant Surgeon General

General Mark W. Clark

Paul I. Robinson Colonel, Medical Corps. Deputy Chief Surgeon

Lieutenant H. R. Anderson

PFC James F. Webb

Henery Wallenstein

James R. Edwards

PFC Richard Clark

Louis Paraga

Chas "Champie" Elder

John P. Ruth Jr.

Howard Shaver

Belvin Kroger

James Deverux

Bill Krogfry

Geraldine "Jerry" Pratt

Frank J. Slenski

Leroy Davidson

Deloris Davidson

Mrs. Lawrence Cooper

Mrs. John Mitchell

Marilyn Melacon

Barbara Law

Edith Alrich

Norman Loomis

Maurice Loomis

Floyd E. Hunt

First Lt. Arthur E. Blake

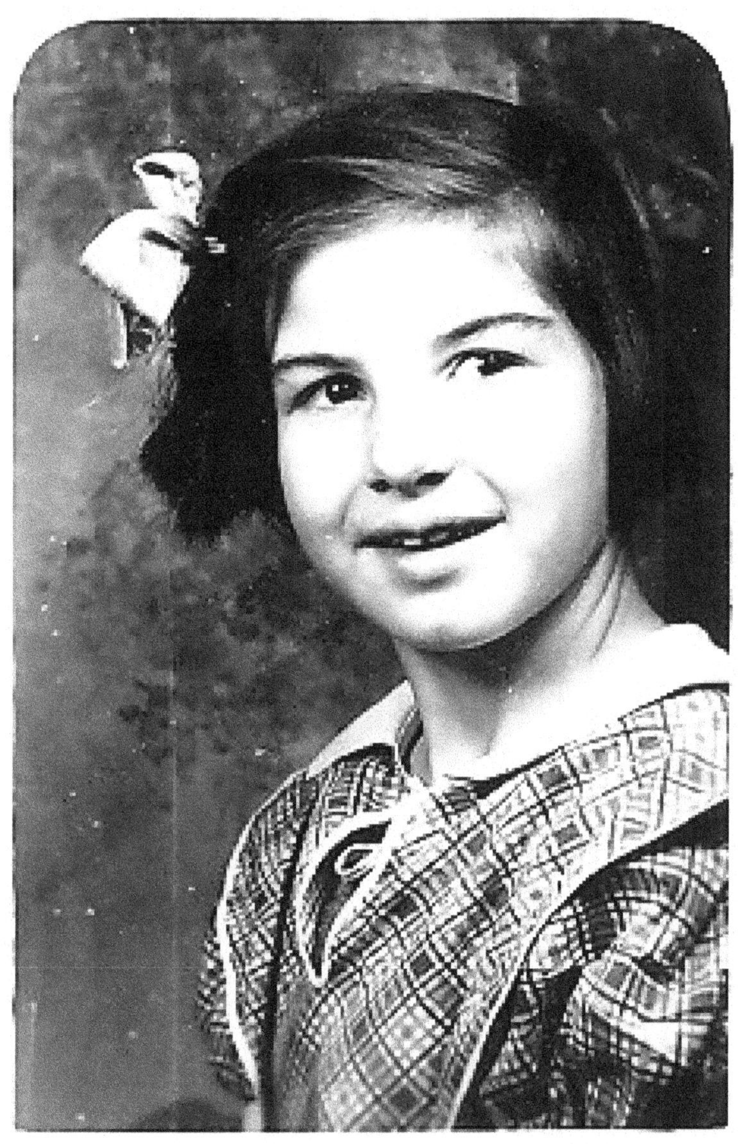

Betty Lou Ross -Hunt

Betty Lou Ross - Hunt was born in Middleton, Idaho, April 1, 1934

Parents are Alma Lea "Ward" Ross and Franklin John Ross.

Betty was the next to the youngest of eight children. Betty was the youngest of the girls. She had three older sisters Dorothy "Dot", and Camilla "Celie". Her older brothers were Franklin Jr. "Frankie", Guy William "Bill", Jack "Eddie", and Fredrick "Freddie", and her younger brother John "Johnny".

I want to start by a brief introduction of the scrap book and later will return to the contents with original letters and the words of those soldiers.

Top left to right: Dorothy, Alma, Camilla, Frank Jr., Frank Sr.

Bottom: John, Jack, Betty, Fred, John

The "Scrap Book of Burnt Offerings" and a better look at its cover. I was astonished at what I found going through this magnificent old burnt scrap book. Inside I found a treasure of pictures and correspondence from soldiers and even a few Generals. General Mark W. Clark and most exciting for me was the acknowledgement from General MacArthur.

Later in this book I will have some entries from another scrap book.

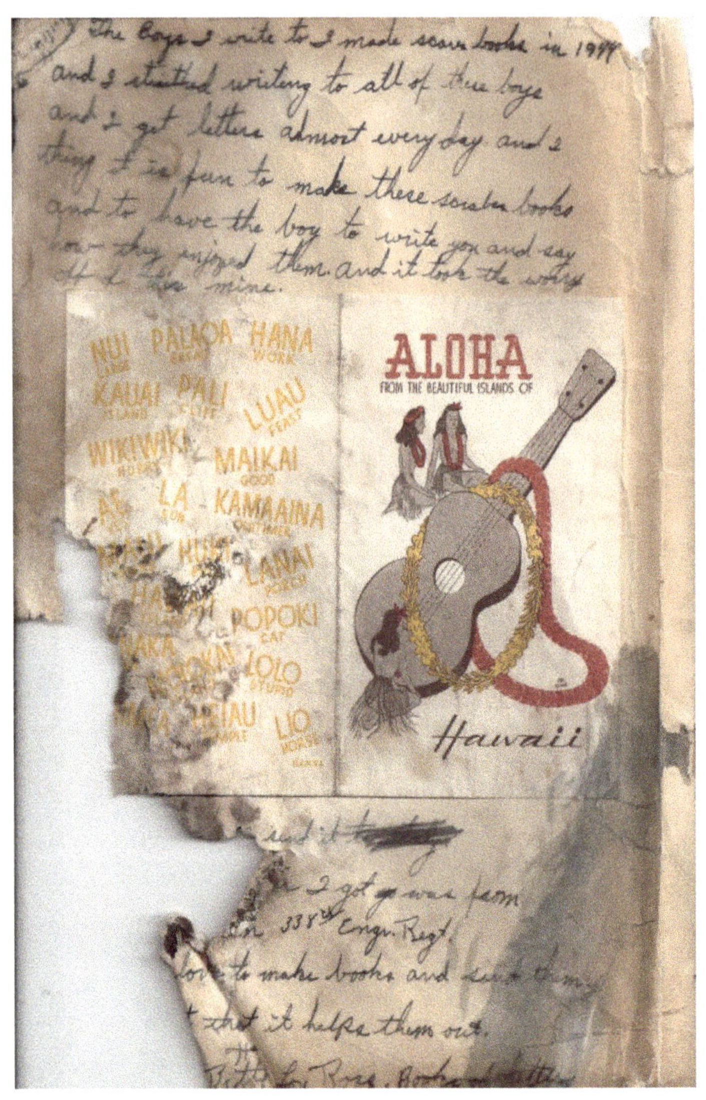

The boys I write to I made scrap books in 1944
And I started writing to all of these boys and I got letters almost everyday.
And I thing it is fun to make these scrap books and to have the boy to write you and say
how they enjoyed them and it took the worry off of this mine
Send it….
I got was from 338th Engr. Regt.
Love to make books and send them…
That it helps them out
Betty Lou Ross Book of Letters

sailors who have enjoyed her scrap
books.

Dear Betty:

I have received your beautiful
Valentine and want to thank you
for your thoughtfulness in sending
it to me. I particularly appreciated
the note you had written on the
back of the card. It is fine to know
that you are devoting the time
that so many children use for play
to this worthwhile task. I will let
you know when the scrap books
reach me, and will see that they
are delivered to some hospital. Our
sick and wounded soldiers will be
delighted to get them. They are always looking for something original and different in their reading matter and your books will fill
that wish.

Your family is making a big contribution toward the war effort,
with four members in the armed
forces. I know how you are looking forward to the day when the
war has been won and they can
return home again. We will continue to do all in our power to
hasten that day.

Thanking you again, and with
best wishes, I am,

Sincerely,
Mark W. Clark,
Lieutenant General, USA,
Commanding.

Climbing fences and playing around was what Betty Lou Ross enjoyed. There was not a lot to do in a small town like New Meadows, Idaho. She loved to be adventurous. She told me a story about what happened this day.

Betty slipped off the fence hitting the ground like so many other times, but not before lodging a huge splinter in her leg. The splinter was so big she would not let her folks even touch her leg.

They waited for her to fall asleep and then held her down and took out the "log" buried deep in her leg.

Photos of some war envelopes, clippings, and pictures from the scrap book.

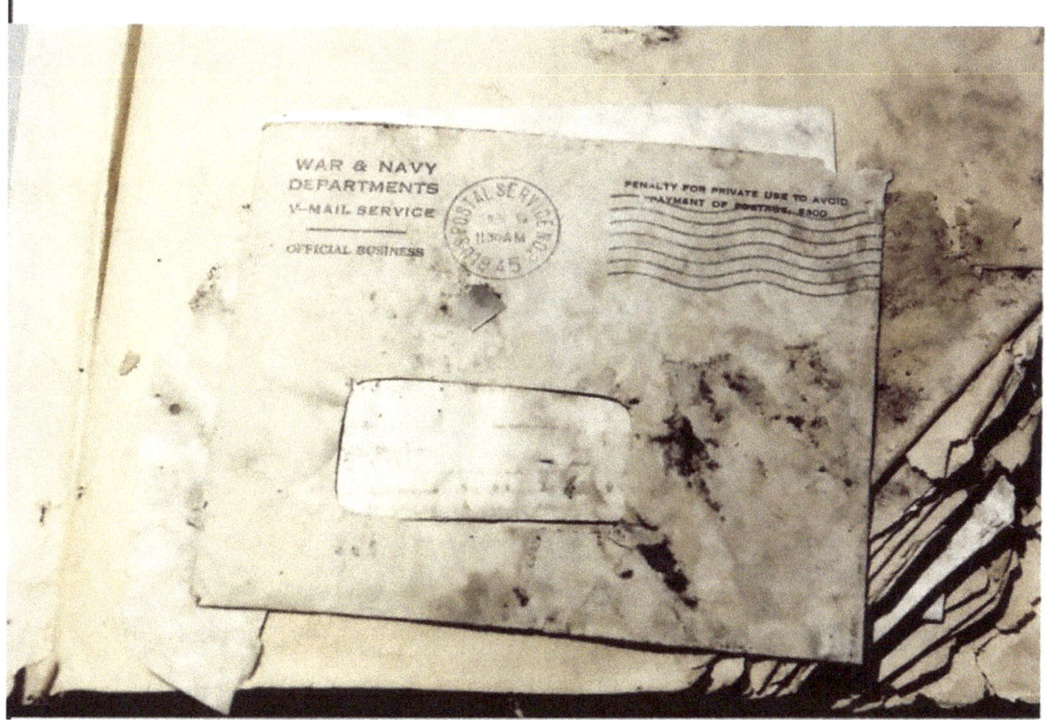

Coming in on a prayer

Betty's mom and dad; Franklin John Ross and Alma Lea Ross, Papa and Nanny as they were called by their grandchildren and family members. Betty's dad served in WWI.

By the year Betty was born 1934 the Great Depression was still ongoing. Food was rationed and luxuries such as sugar were likened to gold. Her home was a buzz from all the activity her mother was causing. Alma Ross was acting along with other members of the community to help those less fortunate. Supplies were used to make various foods and treats for families and their children. Cakes, cookies, cured hams were just a few of the items sent off in gift baskets.

Betty along with her siblings around her age were told to help deliver these baskets and she had a hard time trying to figure out why they were getting food and her family was doing without. As time went on and her brothers were going into the military and serving their country, she was starting to get the feeling of patriotism and could sense the urgency that was flowing in her community. She learned the lesson of giving.

WWII started around 1941 and people could only watch in horror as one by one their men were being sent off to fight. And those unable to fight were hated and scorn. Men not able to go were given a sticker to place in their window; it stated they were 4 F (**4-F** - Not Qualified for Military Service due to medical reasons.) If a window had this it seemed to excuse the man inside from not participating in the war, but still left a very dismal feeling for their families. Betty reveled in the fact that the family had come from a long line of patriotic men and women. As she watched her brothers go off to war and heard stories from her father, his brothers and her mother's brother she wanted to make a difference of her own. Betty noticed people in the community getting involved in many ways. She wanted to be a part of the campaign.

Betty was a volunteer for the ground observer corps of the Aircraft Warning Service (AWS), taking her turn watching for enemy aircraft. She had a letterman's jacket from Meadows High and sported wings she had earned for this service.

The Ross family was a logging family that worked and moved around with the company in West Central Idaho. They lived in Idaho City, Old Macgregor, Cabarton, and finally settled in New Meadows with J. I. Morgan. Prior to J. I. Morgan the logging company was named B. P. L. Co. J. I. Morgan had Mechanical Engineers that worked for him back in 1930; they were a part of the B. P. L. Co. in Cabarton, Idaho.

Early years of Mr. Morgan and his Mechanical Engineers, in Cabarton, Idaho May 1930; they were a part of the BPL Co. at that time.

Logging fleet in New Meadows, Idaho

This is a picture of mom, Betty on the left, her mom Alma and two of her brothers Fred and Johnny.

Betty pictures here with three of her brothers, right to left

Jack (Ed), Betty, Fred, John.

Bettys mom and dad at their home in New Meadows, Idaho

P.F.C Frank E. Ross Jr. Army 123rd Infantry. He suffered severe "shell shock" today called PTSD
Uncle Frank Did Maintenance on Heavy Equipment for J.I. Morgan

Wife Jean, children Gary Dryer, Mary Jane, Robert (Bob), Mike, Barbara, Nancy, John

Aug. 10, 1945

Pfc Frank Ross of New Meadows Gets Citation

Pfc. Franklin E. Ross of New Meadows, has been awarded the Combat Infantryman's Badge for exemplary performance of duty in the action against the Japs. He has been previously awarded the Expert Infantryman's badge, given for meeting the highest standards of the American infantryman, according to a communication from the 33rd division headquarters on Luzon.

Pfc. Ross is a veteran of three campaigns and since February has been participating in the Philippines liberation campaign, seeing action in the rugged, mountainous regions of Northern Luzon. He is eligible to wear the Asiatic-Pacific Overseas ribbon with two battle stars and the Philippines Liberation ribbon with one battle star. Pfc. Ross, who is with the 123rd infantry, entered the army October 12, 1942.

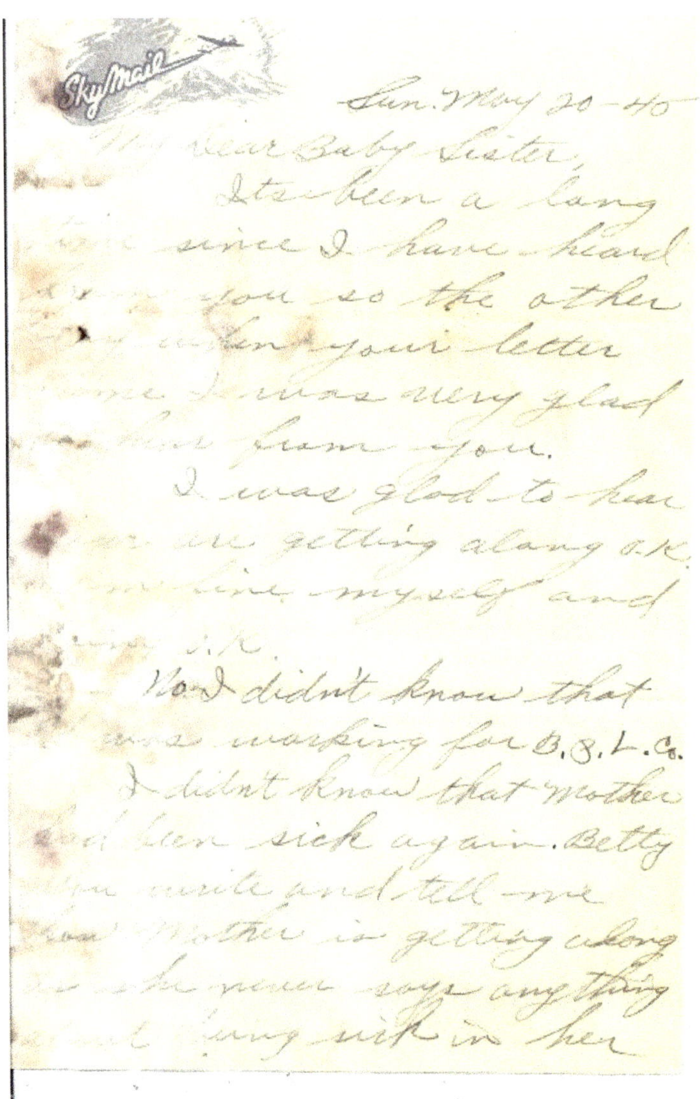

From Brother Franklin E. Ross May 20, 1945

Page 1

My Dear Baby Sister,

It's been a long time since I have heard from you so the other day when your letter came I was very glad to hear from you.

I was glad to hear you are getting along ok. I am fine myself and am ok.

No I didn't know that Ed was working for B.P.L. Co.

I didn't know that Mother had been sick again. Betty you write and tell me how Mother is getting along as she never says anything about being sick in her

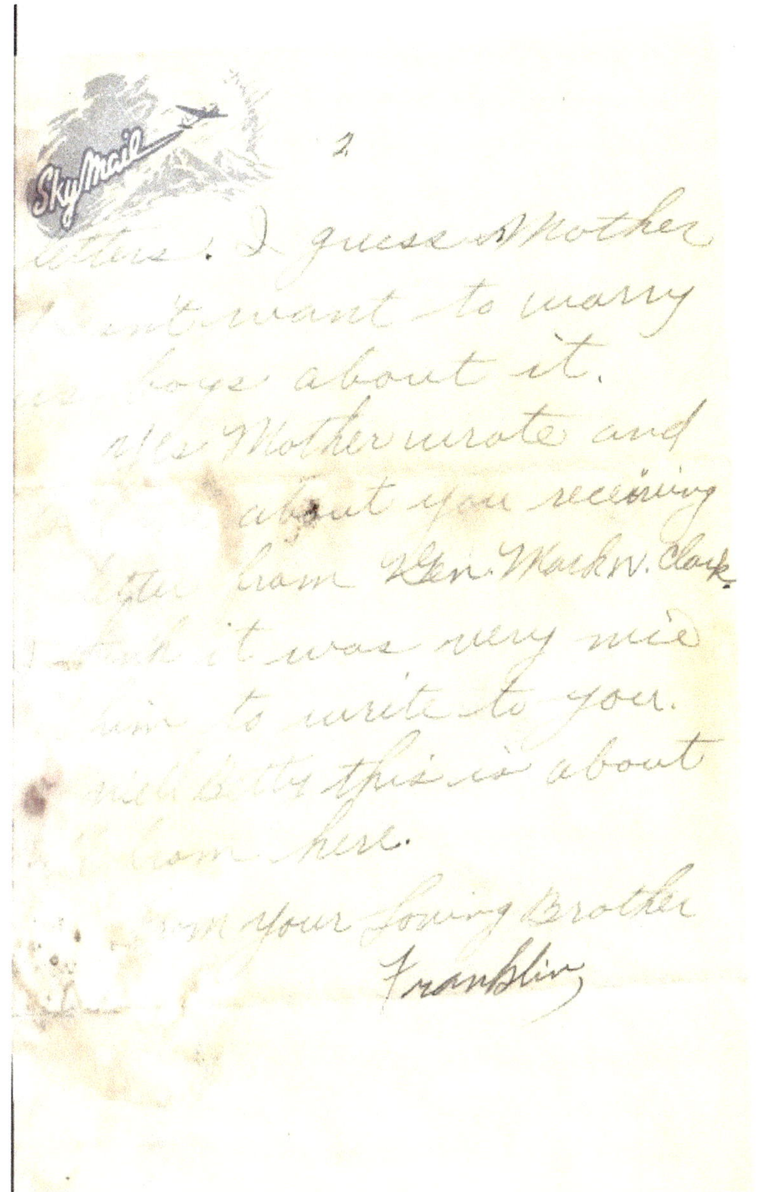

From Brother Franklin E. Ross May 20, 1945

Page 2

letters. I guess Mother doesn't want to worry us boys about it.

Yes Mother wrote and told me about you receiving a letter from General Mark W. Clark.

I think it was very nice of him to write to you.

Well Betty this is about all from here.

From your Loving Brother

Franklin

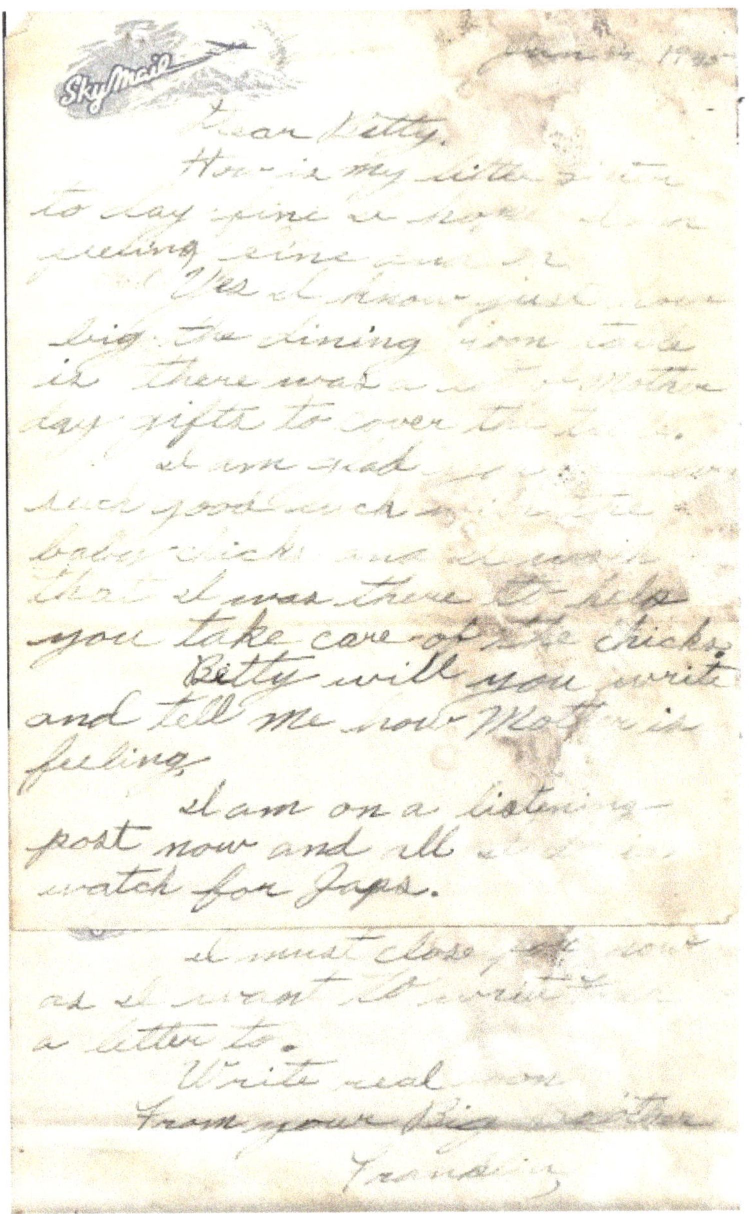

From Brother Franklin E. Ross June 4, 1945

Dear Betty,

How is my little sister to day fine I hope I am feeling fine and ok.

Yes I know just how big the dining room table is there was a lot of Mothers day gifts to cover the table.

I am glad you are having such good luck with the baby chicks and I wish I was there to help you take care of the chicks.

Betty will you write and tell me how Mother is feeling.

I am on a listening post now and all I do is watch for Japs.

I must close for now as I want to write Fred a letter to.

Write real soon

From your Big Brother

Franklin

From Brother Franklin E. Ross June 21, 1945

Page 1

My Dear littler Sister

How are you tonite Betty fine I hope and pray, I am feeling fine and O.K. How is Mother feeling now.

Say Betty did you know I was located near Bogio the summer capital of the Philippines on Luzon. We were only allowed to tell you this a short time ago. We are a high up in the mountains here and that makes it very cool. I like the weather very much. We live in tents and have

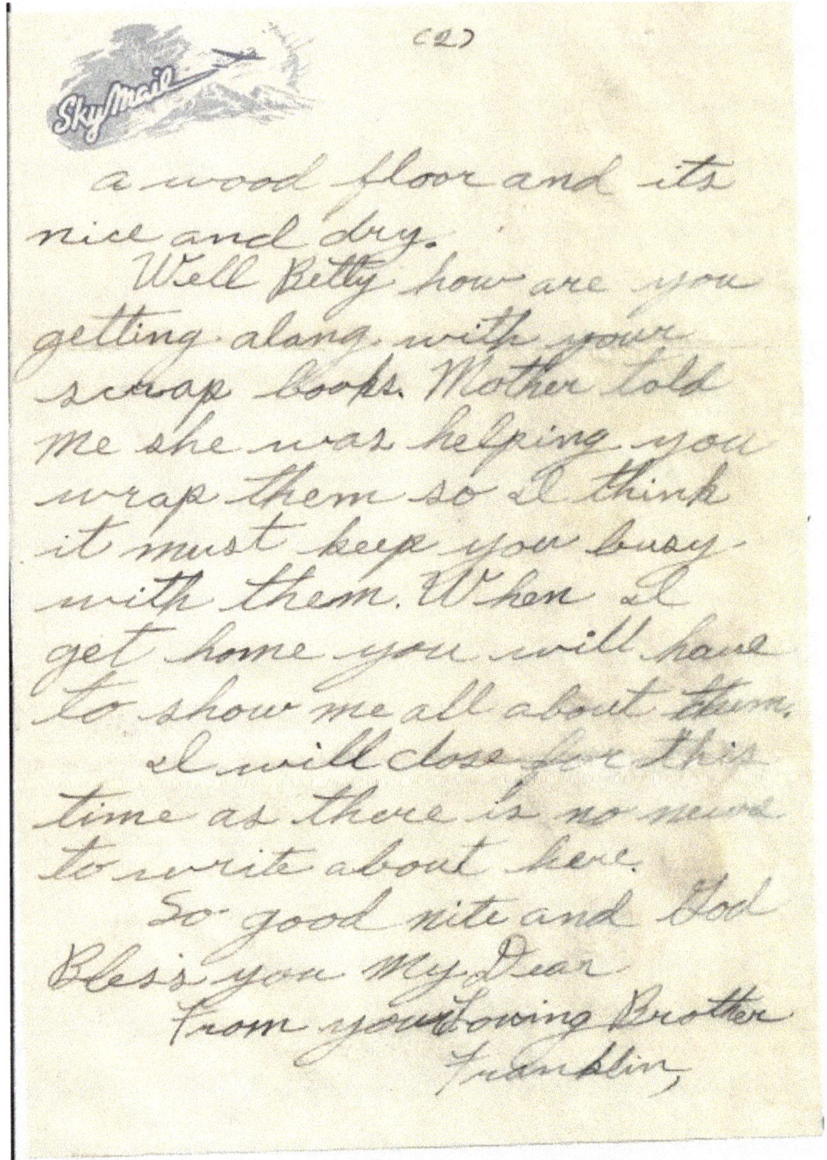

From Brother Franklin E. Ross June 21, 1945

Page 2

A wood floor and its nice and dry.

Well Betty how are you getting along with your scrap books. Mother told me she was helping you wrap them so I think it must keep you busy with them. When I get home you will have to show me all about them.

I will close for this time as there is no more to write about here.

So good nite and God Bless you My Dear

From your Loving Brother

Franklin

From Brother Franklin E. Ross July 15, 1945

Page 1

Dear Betty

I just received two letters from you and glad to get them. How is my little sis today feeling fine I hope and pray. I am feeling fine and O.K.

I go to the show nearly every nite as there is nothing else to do.

I am glad you are catching a lot of fish.

I don't go fishing myself but the natives go fishing every morning in the ocean. We only live a short ways from

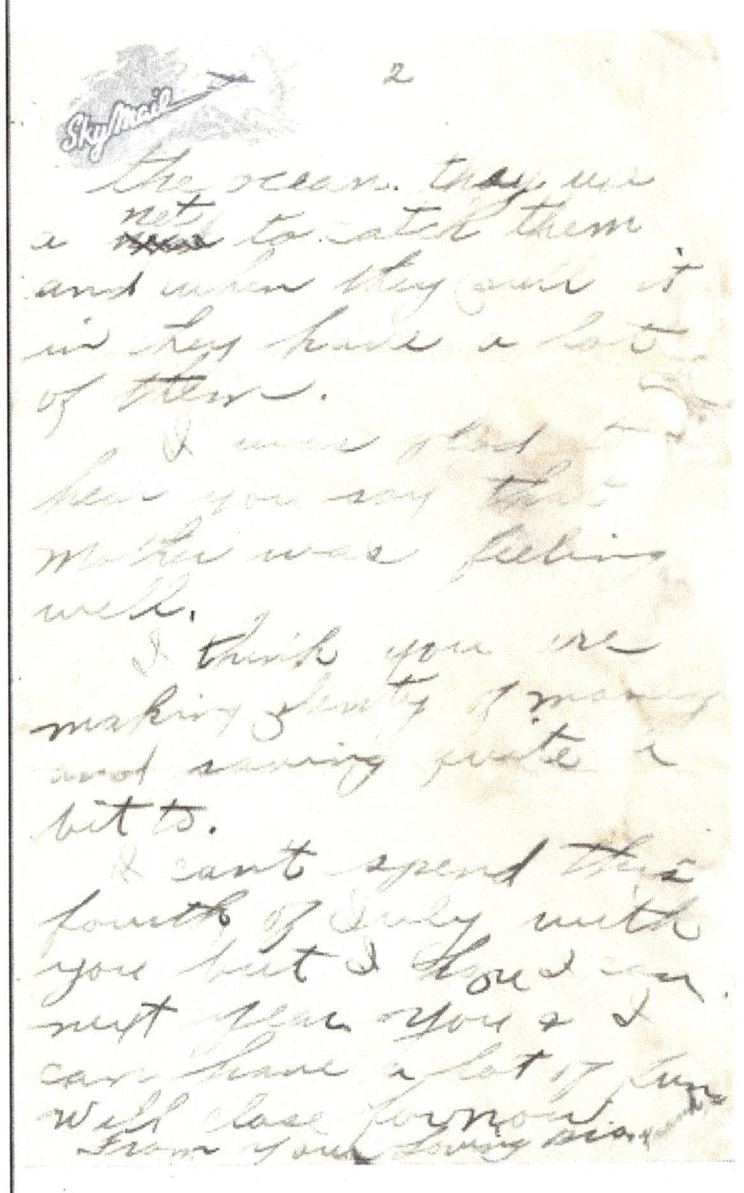

From Brother

Franklin E. Ross

July 15, 1945

Page 2

The ocean. They use a net to catch them and when they pull it in they have a lot of them.

I was glad to hear you say Mother was feeling well.

I think you are making plenty of money and saving quite a bit to.

I can't spend this fourth of July with you but I hope I can next year you and I can have a lot of fun.

Will close for now

From your Loving Bro Frank

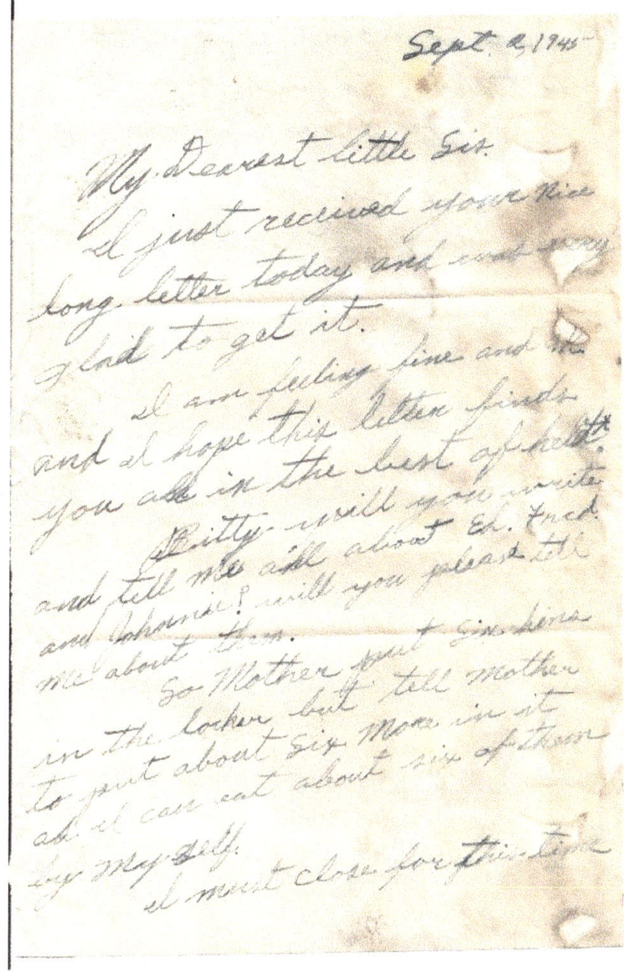

From Brother Franklin E. Ross Sept. 2, 1945

My Dearest little Sis

I just received your nice long letter today and was very glad to get it.

I am feeling fine and O.K. and I hope this letter finds you all in the best of health.

Betty will you write and tell me all about Ed, Fred and Johnny? Will you please tell me about them.

So Mother put six hens in the locker but tell Mother to put about six more in it as I can eat about six of them by myself.

I must close for this time as I am running out of news to write about. So write real soon

Lots of Love From your

Big Brother

Franklin

Betty's oldest sister Dorothy "Dot" Lea Ross and her husband Warren Loomis

Warren Loomis Navy Front Gunner USS McCord

Uncle Warren was a Logging truck driver for J.I. Morgan Logging

Wife moms sister Dorothy (Dot), Children: Baby Del, Veldora "Doddie", Connie

Loomis Brothers and Loomis Family

Warren, Norman, and Maurice   Parents Vida. And Clarence Loomis

WARREN LOOMIS
USS MCCORD
WWII NAVY VETERAN

Leroy and Deloris Davidson, friends of Warren and Dorothy Loomis

They lived together while in California during Warren and Leroy's time there.

Deloris wrote Betty several letters.

Deloris Davidson
Oct. 2, 1945   San Diego, Ca.

Dear Betty Lou,

Received your nice letter and was very glad to hear from you. Thanks a million for the pictures honey, it was very sweet of you to send it.

The weather here is sure hot and sticky through the day but its been cool nights which helps a lot.

I cant say as I like California, not in San Diego anyways just to large a city for me.

Dorothy, Warren, Leroy, and me rented us a 4 room house last Sunday and moved in. It isn't a bit nice but its better than living in a Hotel and having to eat all our meals out.

We do all our own cooking now which Dorothy and I love to do.

The boys are close to the base now which makes it nice too.

Dot and I walked every where yesterday trying to find an alarm clock, finally found one but we were sure tired last night.

We haven't did a thing today but

Deloris Davidson
Oct. 2, 1945
San Diego, Ca.

Page 2

Lay around, looking at comic books and eating.

Dot got a letter from your Mother today, she is planning soon to come after Veldora.

How is your Mother, Dad and the boys Tell them all I said hello.

Was sorry to hear your brothers orders changed and that he wont be home when he thought.

I know it was a big disappointment to all of you.

Well honey there isn't much to write about so will close for now.

Thanking you again for the picture and hoping to hear from you soon.

Lots of love,

Deloris

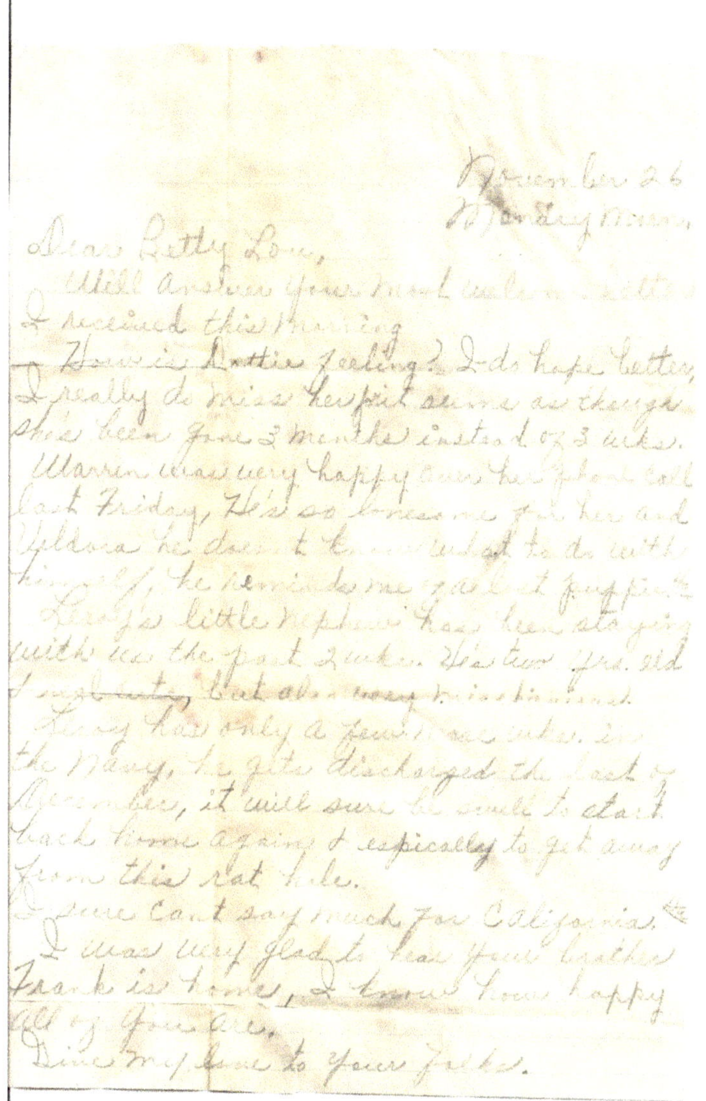

Deloris Davidson   Nov. 26, 1945
Monday Morn

Dear Betty Lou,

Will answer your most welcome letter I received this morning.

How is Dottie feeling? I do hope better. I really do miss her for it seems as though shes been gone 3 months instead of 3 weeks. Warren was very happy over her phone call last Friday, He's so lonesome for her and Veldora he doesn't know what to do with himself, he reminds me of a lost puppy. Ha

Leroys little nephew has been staying with us the past 2 wks. He's two yrs. Old and real cute, but also very mischievous.

Leroy has only a few more wks. in the Navy, he gets discharged the last week in December, it will sure be swell to start back home again and especially to get away from this rat hole.

I sure cant say much for California. Ha

I was very glad to hear your brother Frank is home, I know how happy all of you are.

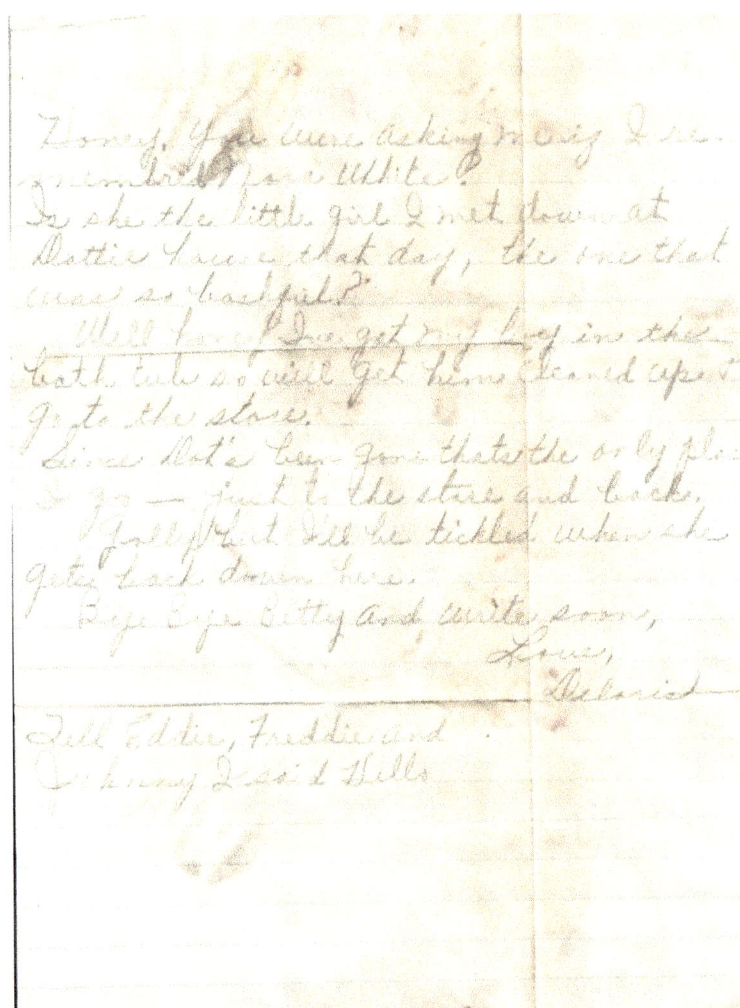

Deloris Davidson
Nov. 26, 1945
Monday Morn

Page 2

Honey you were asking me if I remembered Nora White? Is she that little girl I met down at Dotties house that day, the one that was so bashful?

Well honey Ive got my boy in the bath tub get him cleaned up and go to the store.

Since Dot's been gone that the only place I go_____ just to the store and back.

Golly but I'll be tickled when she gets back down here.

Bye Bye Betty and write soon,

Love,

Deloris

Tell Eddie, Freddie and Johnny I said Hello

Dec. 15

Dear Betty Lou,

Well honey this is Sat. morning, Warren & Leroy just left for the Base.

Will answer your letter I received this wk.

This is my last letter to write in Calif. (Thank Heavens).

Yes, honey Im a very happy girl today, as Leroy goes to Camp Eliott this morning for his discharge

We'll be leaving for Kans. next wk, And hope to be their for Xmas.

Im anxious to get started for home but I really hate the thoughts of leaving

Dec. 15, 1945

Friendly Christmas Greetings

A greeting filled
with all the joy
That friendly thoughts
can bring,
To wish you, now
and all the time,

The Best
of Everything.
Love,
Deloris And Leroy
Davidson

Betty's brother Guy William "Bill" Ross

Guy William Ross   Army Corp. of Engineers
Sawyer for J.I. Morgan Logging, and Rancher Walking W Ranch New Meadows, ID

Wife Venita (Nita) children Micki

Name Ross was spelt wrong in the article

Pvt. Harry E. Ralston of Boise, Corp. Guy W. Rose of New Meadows and Pvt. Dominic N. DeGullio of Pingree are members of the 38th engineer general service regiment which recently concluded a brillant chapter of its history by opening the obliterated part of Leghorn, Italy, to Allied convoys.

Recuperating at a hospital in England from wounds received last December on the Western front is First Lt. Arthur E. Blake, son of Elmer L. Blake of Boise. The lieutenant's wife and daughter reside at Fort Smith, Ark. It had previously been erroneously reported the Boise's wife and son lived at Fort Smith.

Betty's brother Jack "Ed" Ross Army

Served in 3 campaigns in Korea, and 2 in Vietnam. From what I recall he spoke 7 languages and served with a part of the CIA. He was part of the Mountain Guards that infiltrated mountain villages in Vietnam. His son Bradley said he was awarded the Purple Heart and one for Bravery when he was shot in his leg.

Wife Della, children Marcy, Brad, Cathy, Angie, Mary Margaret

Years later Jack and Betty's youngest brother Johnny would meet up and cause quite a stir when two brothers were in the same camp. This made the world news, I remember watching TV one night and seeing it come up on the news cast.

John Ross   Jack "Ed" Ross

John L. Ross The Youngest
Wife Toshi (Okinawan) children Tommy, Wesley, Bobby

Did not serve in WW 11
Retired Army Ranger
Served Korea, and Vietnam

Army Ranger Retired Military

NEW MEADOWS
By Mrs. Harold Bannon

Miss Kathryn Richmond arrived home from Portland recently, where she spent the winter months.

Mrs. Ray Brooks and daughter, Allene; Mrs. Hubert Higgins and daughter, Virginia, attended the Mothers' Day banquet at McCall Monday evening, given by the Jobs Daughters, honoring the mothers of the members of the order.

Mr. and Mrs. C. W. Jackson were dinner guests Monday evening of Mr. and Mrs. Frank Ross.

sang and played a very beautiful number. Many useful and appropriate gifts were presented the honored guest. Refreshments concluded a pleasant evening, served by the hostess, Mrs. Farrell, and her co-hostess, Mrs. Laurabelle Posada.

Mrs. Flora Cox of Fruitland, is visiting in the home of her daughter, Mrs. C. V. Loomis.

John Price, daughter, and grandson of Burwell, Nebraska, are visiting the Tom Connor family.

Mrs. Warren Loomis and her daughter were dinner guests of Mr. and Mrs. Ray Forrey Sunday

Mr. and Mrs. W. C. Hollenback and daughter will leave soon for Reno, Nevada. Mr. Hollenback has secured a release from the Boise Payette Lumber company, where he has been employed as a machinist for a number of years.

Eddie Ross was guest of honor at a surprise birthday party at the BPL hall Monday evening, on his 16th birthday. Thirty-two guests were present. Prizes for the best stories told were awarded to Miss Dimple Green and Jimmie Higgins, for which they received free tickets to the show. Second prizes went to Miss Barbara Bedel and LaWayne Rich, each receiving a free milk shake. Consolation prizes went to Delbert Middlekauf and Miss Viola Rich, who received free cokes. Eddie received many lovely birfthday gifts. A very enjoyable time was had. Hostesses were Mrs. Millie Forrey, Mrs. Dot Loomis, Mrs. Wilma Carr and Mrs. Frank Ross.

From Brother Jack Edwin "Ed" Ross March 21, 1949

Page 1

Dearest Sis,

Hi honey, how are you feeling this afternoon? Fine and in the best of health I do hope. I am feeling fine. Gee today sure is nice out. It hasn't rained now for a couple of days but it is still quite hot.

I received your most welcome letter and sure was glad to hear from you again. Say Honey are you going back to California this summer. I sure hope so because now I see that it isn't a bad state at all. But when you do have fun for me. So Bill is really getting into the racket "?" is it on the level. I've just been wondering. I know Bill

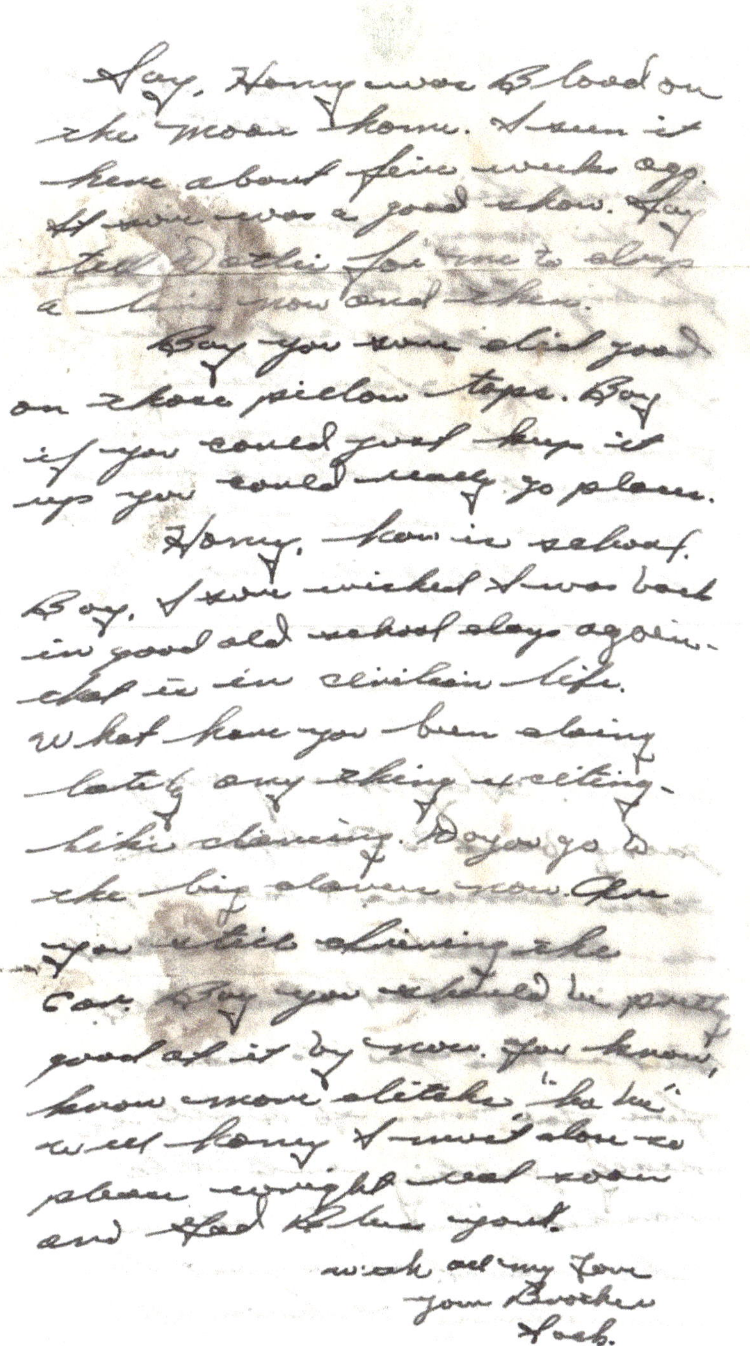

From Brother Jack Edwin "Ed" Ross March 21, 1949

Page 2

Say, honey was the blood on the moon home. I seen it here about five weeks ago. It sure was a good show. Say tell Dodie for me to drop a line now and then.

Boy you sure did good on those pillow tops. Boy if you could just keep it up you could really go places.

Honey, how is school.

Boy, sure wish I was back in good old school days again. That is in civilian life.

What have you been doing lately any thing exciting, like dancing. Do you go to the big dances now. Are you still driving the car. Boy you should be pretty good at it by now. You know, know more stitches "ha ha"

Well honey I must close so please wright real soon and God Bless you.

With all my Love

Your Brother

Jack

From Brother Jack Edwin "Ed" Ross May 2, 1952

Hi Honey- I received your most welcomed letters and sure was glad to be hearing from the best Sister on earth. I'm sorry that I have been so poor on answering your letter but I really will try to do better in the future. I Promise. How are you feeling this afternoon? I hope your in the best of health and getting along great. I was sure glad to hear that you are having fun, Honey because you are only young once and you want to make it good. I know that I do.

How is school coming along? Fine, I do hope. I guess you will be out for Summer Vacation soon. Do you know what you are going to do yet this summer. Are you going to work at McCall. I hope you do get a job away from New Meadows for a while. How is Mother feeling? Wonderful, I really do hope. Has Mother got the Present yet. I do hope you all like it. It did'nt go to well for the hair cut but you know there was'nt much I could do about it being it was all most cut off.

I got my name in on a school back east. I sure hope I get it. I am qualified for it. There can only be one out of the company that can go.I sure hope I get to go. But there is a lot of Sgt's that intered there names also, also one Lt. in the outfit. So if I get it, it would just be sheer luck.

I got a letter from Venita Thomas the other day. Tell her I will write her a letter one of these days as soon as I can. So, women why don't you send me some pictures of your self any way. I sure would like some. OK, so I will be expecting some soon. Got to close for now a Prisoner just came in. Will finish this letter after I have Processed him in.

Well, here I am again-and doing a poor job of it by the looks of the spelling. If I don't go to school I am going to come home on a pass this July for a few days. It will be good to be home again.

Boy, If this keep's up I will never get this letter finished. I just had to get the Prisoners Mail Registered. Boy, I hate that job. Oh hell I wish it was five O'clock for I could go to the barracks and lay down for a bet.

Say, Honey tell Mother thanks a million for the package. I really liked it. Cigs and gum is one thang us fellow in the Army need and run out of more than anything else I know of.

Well, Honey I must close for now for I have to get some more work done.

Please write real soon and I will do the same I promise.

Good night and god bless you always.

All my love always

Your Brother

Eddie

PS Give Mother a great big kiss for me.

Brother Fredrick Donald Ross "Fred"

Fredrick Ross Army   Heavy Equipment Operator and Mechanic

He was sent to atomic bomb blast testing. As well as Pahnpei during BRAVO Nucular Bomb test site, the largest Thermonuclear bomb ever tested. He was located in an underground cement bunker. Died years later of nuclear radiation poisoning from Eniwetok Kwajalein.

Wife Peggy "Native Hawaiian" , children Sylvia, Amy, Peggy, Ipo, Jack, Lani

Betty's sister Camilla "Celie" Lucille Ross and her husband Marion Connor

Marion Connor Navy Cook"Galley"

Wife Celie "moms Sister", children Claudia, Ross, Linda

Wedding Photos and News Article

MR. AND MRS. MARION H. CONNER were married Sept. 30 at the home of the bride's uncle and aunt in Huntington Park, Calif. The bride is the former Miss Camilla L. Ross of New Meadows.

NEW MEADOWS COUPLE WED IN CALIFORNIA

NEW MEADOWS—Miss Camilla Lucille Ross and Marion Howard Conner, seaman third class, U.S.N., both of New Meadows, were married Sept. 30 by the Rev. Francis L. Bennett, Presbyterian minister, at the home of the bride's uncle and aunt, Mr. and Mrs. C. S. DeLong, in Huntington Park, Calif.

The bride wore a brown 'suit with brown accessories and a corsage of orchids. She is the daughter of Mr. and Mrs. Frank Ross of New Meadows.

The bridegroom is the son of Mr. and Mrs. Thomas Conner of New Meadows.

The bride is a graduate of the Meadows Valley high school and was employed at the Stockwell store. The bridegroom was an employe of the Boise Payette lumber company before joining the Navy and is now stationed at San Pedro, Calif.

Betty also became very involved with this program in New Meadows and watched for enemy planes that might try to fly into the United States by way of Canada. Quite a coupe for Betty because members were all boys, her name is not mentioned here, I have seen the pin she received for her service.

Boise, Idaho, Thursday

Newly Formed Boise Air Scouts To Hold Meet

Jaycee Sponsored Group Will Assemble At Bishop Tuttle House

The recently-organized Boise air scout squadron will meet today at 7:30 p. m. at the Bishop Tuttle house for instruction on the construction of model airplanes, given by personnel from Gowen field.

Ross Simmons, squadron leader, Wednesday requested that all boys 15 years of age or older who are interested in joining the air scout group to telephone him at 2188 or Capt. R. G. Abb at Gowen field, extension 263.

A new air scout building at the Boise barracks to accommodate 50 members will be ready for occupancy soon where lectures will be given the boys on instruments for flying, navigation, aerodynamics, weather, gliding and soaring, combat lectures and aircraft engines.

The work is not flying itself, Simmons explained, but is instruction on all phases of aviation with special emphasis placed on model construction and competitive meets. The group has already competed in one glider contest and many excellent flights were made, he added.

The troop is sponsored by the Boise junior chamber of commerce, with Stanley R. Rhees assisting Squadron Leader Simmons. Vernon Fry is the senior boy leader.

"Betty Lou, I am very happy to know that you are the type of girl that we are over here fighting for. So God bless you, Betty Lou and thank you for sending your very nice book. It helps more than you will ever know. Again I say God bless you."

"Your friend, Pfc. James F. Webb, Ren. Co. 805, T. D. Bn, APO 464 care Post Master, New York. Home address, 52 Birmingham Terrace, Toledo, (5) Ohio."

A second letter Betty Lou received is this one:

"Dear Betty: I received your scrap book the other day and it was swell. Also the nicest thing I have received since being overseas. First of all, I spent an hour enjoying every bit of it, as we don't get much to read except month old papers and magazines. After I finished it, I passed it on to your brother, Guy, and although he didn't say much, I knew he enjoyed it as much as I did, especially the snap shots of home. He told me all about them and I know he is proud of you for making such a nice scrap book as he had all the men in the platoon which I am the officer of, look it over so that proves it. After they read it from cover to cover, I packed it up and sent it to an officer up on the fighting front, so by the time you receive this letter, your book will be where you wished it to be sent and will be enjoyed by many soldiers there. So believe me, Betty, all the hard work you put into it was certainly worth while and means so much to all of us over here, to receive things like that.

"Your brother, Guy, is one of my three corporals in my platoon and besides being an excellent soldier, is a swell fellow and wish all my men were like him. He is in fine health and doing a good job. Tell your mother, father, and sister, they can be proud of him, as I think lots of him. So thanks loads. Lt. H. R. Anderson, Co. F. 338th Engrs, APO 782, care Post Master, N. Y."

New Meadows Girl Receives Letters From G. I. Pen Pals

NEW MEADOWS (Special)— Thirteen-year-old Betty Lou Ross has for her pen pals the fightiing doughboys of practically all the fronts.

Most of their letters are written to her from hospital cots, however, for it has been in overseas hospitals that they have first learned of a little girl named Betty Lou.

Wanting to help the war effort some time ago, the New Meadows child made scrapbooks and sent them to our hospitals in Italy and in the South Pacific.

Here is a typical letter of the many she has received. It was written by Pfc. James F. Webb, Toledo, Ohio:

"It may be some time before your scrap book finds its way back to you, so I thought you would like to know how the boys over here in Italy like it.

"There have been 109 soldiers' names from several states entered in the back of your book, and that in itself should show you what they think of it.

"I have been overseas 23 months and I think it's the finest thing anyone has done for the soldier that has no one to turn to when he is sick. It helps the soldier to realize that someone back home is thinking about him.

"Betty Lou, I am very happy to know that you are the type of little girl that we are over here fighting for.

"So God bless you, Betty Lou, and thank you for sending your very nice book; it helps more than you will ever know. Again I say, God bless you."

Dear Pauline

I taken a package of Scrapbooks to McCall. and mail them to a General as Bitty had his request.

The package was 47 inches weighted more then 5 lbs.

The Postmaster looked it up and where a package is sent for the Wellfare and morals of our Soldiers and "a approval" it will go Through.

Mrs Ross.

Some time will you please look this up as Bitty has General MacArthur approval, also - and she is to send books every 2 months.

Boise, Idaho

June 9, 1945

ECF:dc

Postmaster,
New Meadows, Idaho

My dear Postmaster:

In your letter of June 6th, you enclosed a letter from
Mrs. Ross concerning scrap books sent in the mails to overseas
destinations which are over in weight and size and she states
in her letter that special permission has been received because these articles for the welfare and morale of the soldiers
and that she has General MacArthur's approval.

Evidently, it is her intention to mail these articles,
which are overweight and oversize for regular packages in the
mail to soldiers and sailors overseas and it is believed that
she intends to mail under the exceptions marked in red pencil
on the attached forms, which are considered parcels for military
agencies when so marked by sender and which are addressed to
certain organizations mentioned therein or to the commanding
officers for morale and welfare of soldiers. It is suggested
that you give copy of the instructions to Mrs. Ross, so that
she can mark her articles for military agencies, which no doubt
will go forward to destination under such title.

Very truly yours,

Harry L. Yost, Postmaster

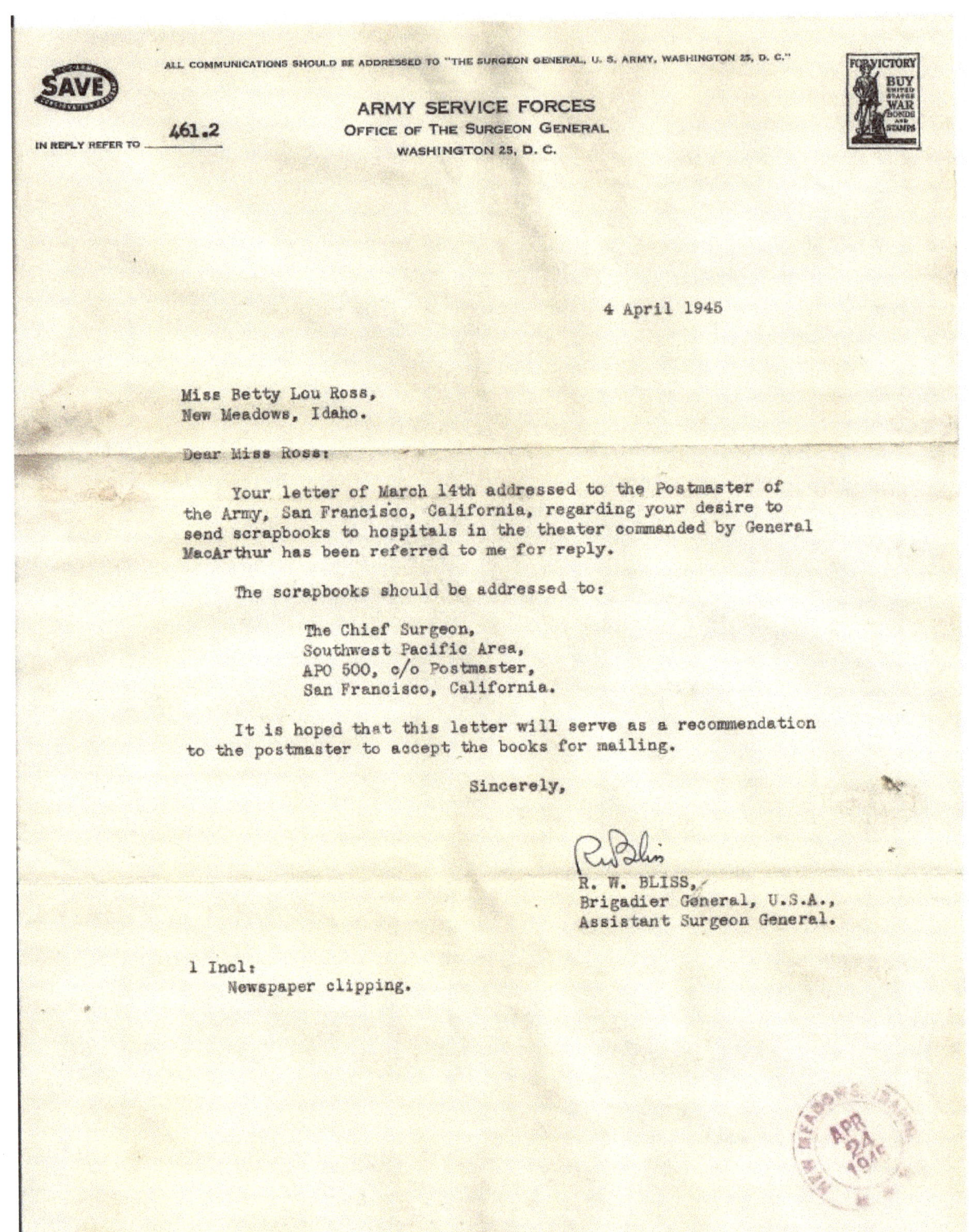

ALL COMMUNICATIONS SHOULD BE ADDRESSED TO "THE SURGEON GENERAL, U. S. ARMY, WASHINGTON 25, D. C."

ARMY SERVICE FORCES
OFFICE OF THE SURGEON GENERAL
WASHINGTON 25, D. C.

IN REPLY REFER TO 461.2

FOR VICTORY
BUY
UNITED STATES
WAR
BONDS
AND
STAMPS

4 April 1945

Miss Betty Lou Ross,
New Meadows, Idaho.

Dear Miss Ross:

Your letter of March 14th addressed to the Postmaster of the Army, San Francisco, California, regarding your desire to send scrapbooks to hospitals in the theater commanded by General MacArthur has been referred to me for reply.

The scrapbooks should be addressed to:

The Chief Surgeon,
Southwest Pacific Area,
APO 500, c/o Postmaster,
San Francisco, California.

It is hoped that this letter will serve as a recommendation to the postmaster to accept the books for mailing.

Sincerely,

R. W. BLISS,
Brigadier General, U.S.A.,
Assistant Surgeon General.

1 Incl:
Newspaper clipping.

This is the war envelope that held letter from General Mark M. Clark. I found this photo of the General among many online.

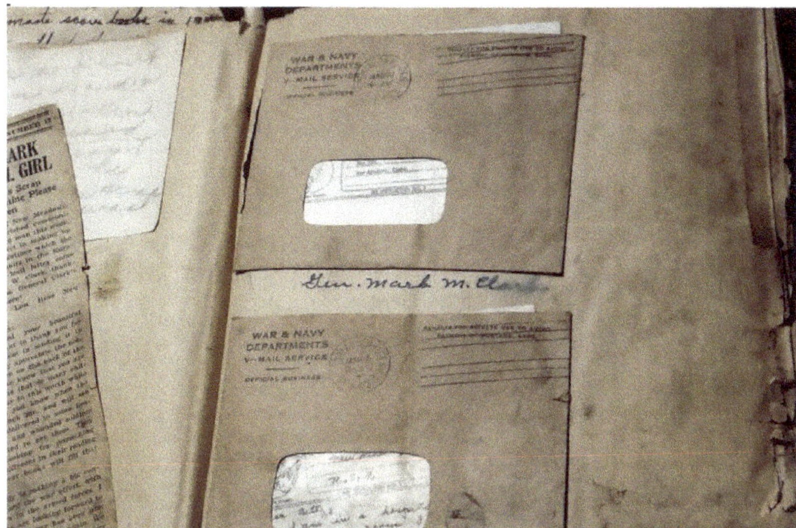

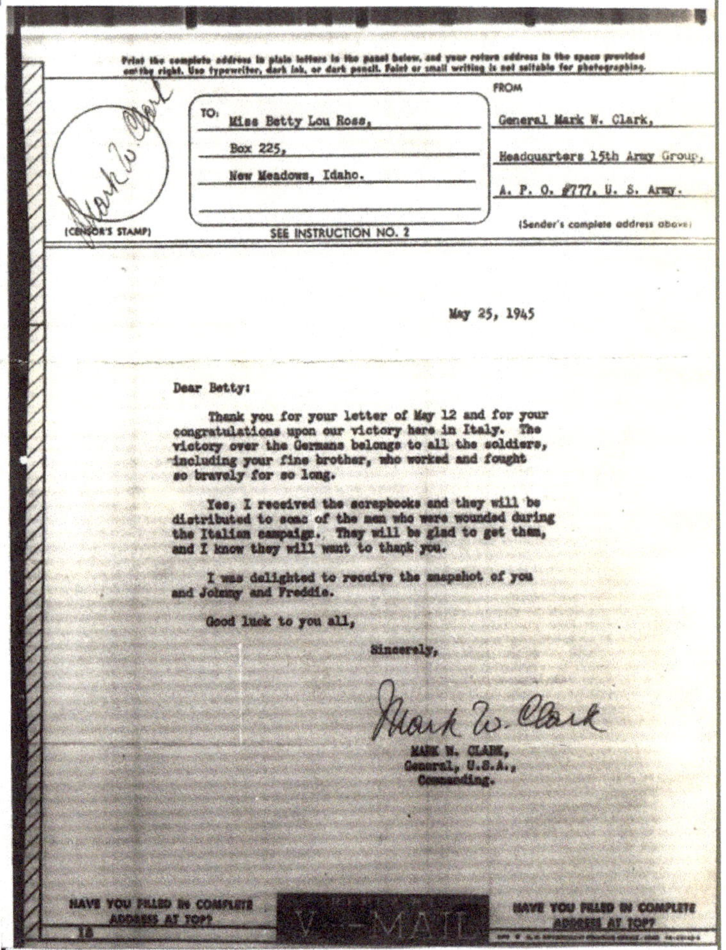

General Mark W. Clark
Headquarters 15th
Army Group
May 25, 1945

Dear Betty,

Thank you for your letter of May 12 and for your congratulations upon our victory here in Italy. The victory over the Germans belongs to all the soldiers, including your fine brother, who worked and fought so bravely for so long.

Yes, I received the scrap books and they will be distributed to some of the men who were wounded during the Italian campaign. They will be glad to get them, and I know they will want to thank you.

I was delighted to receive the snapshot of you and Johnny and Freddie.

Good luck to you all,

Sincerely,

Mark W. Clark
General, U.S.A.
Commanding

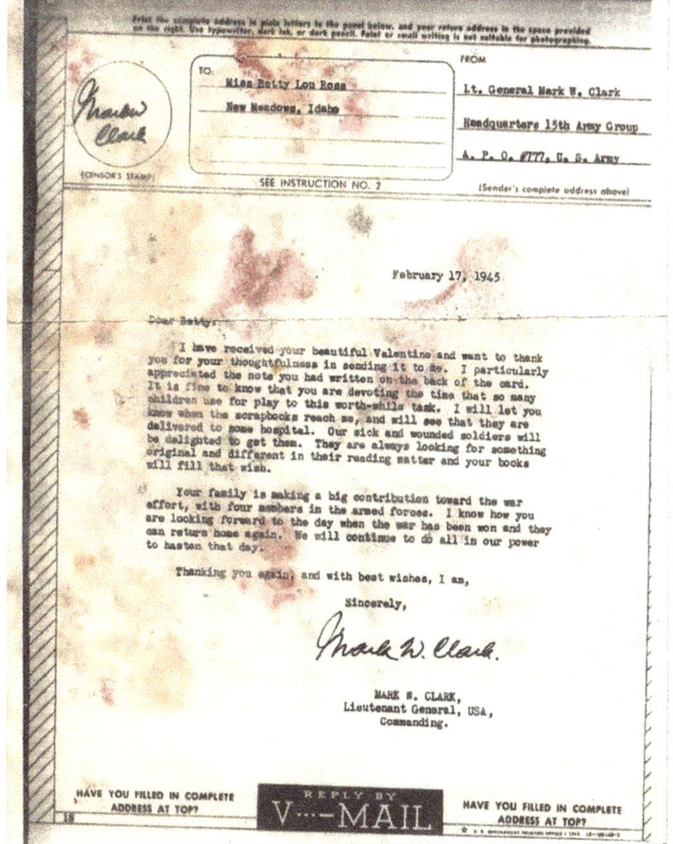

February 17, 1945

Dear Betty:

I have received your beautiful Valentine and want to thank you for your thoughtfulness in sending it to me. I particularly appreciated the note you had written on the back of the card. It is fine to know that you are devoting the time that so many children use for play to this worth-while task. I will let you know when the scrapbooks reach me, and will see that they are delivered to some hospital. Our sick and wounded soldiers will be delighted to get them. They are always looking for something original and different in their reading matter and your books will fill that wish.

Your family is making a big contribution toward the war effort, with four members in the armed forces. I know how you are looking forward to the day when the war has been won and they can return home again. We will continue to do all in our power to hasten that day.

Thanking you again, and with best wishes, I am,

Sincerely,

MARK W. CLARK,
Lieutenant General, USA,
Commanding.

GENERAL CLARK WRITES N. M. GIRL

Betty Lou Ross's Scrap Book and Valentine Please Officers and Men

Betty Lou Ross of New Meadows, received another cherished communication from a fighting man this week, for her one-girl project in making up scrap books and valentines which she sends to different units in the European sectors. A V-Mail letter came from General Mark W. Clark, thanking the young miss. General Clark's letter is printed here:

"To Miss Betty Lou Ross New Meadows, Idaho.

"Dear Miss Betty:

"I have received your beautiful Valentine and want to thank you for your thoughtfulness in sending it to me, I particularly appreciate the note you had written on the back of the card. It is fine to know that you are devoting the time that so many children use for play to this worth while task. I will let you know when the scrap books reach me, and will see that they are delivered to some hospital. Our sick and wounded soldiers will be delighted to get them. They are always looking for something original and different in their reading matter and your books will fill that wish.

"Your family is making a big contribution toward the war effort, with four members in the armed forces. I know how you are looking forward to the day when the war has been won and they can return home again. We will continue to do all in our power to hasten that day.

"Thanking you again, and with best wishes, I am sincerely,

"Mark W. Clark,
Lieutenant General USA,
Commanding."

GENERAL HEADQUARTERS
UNITED STATES ARMY FORCES, PACIFIC
OFFICE OF THE CHIEF SURGEON

A.P.O.   500

16 June 1945

Miss Betty Lou Ross
New Meadows, Idaho

Dear Betty Lou:

The Chief Surgeon has asked me to write you so you would know he has received your nice letter of June 7, 1945. We have not received the three packages of scrap books which you mention in your letter but you may be assured that they will be sent to one of our hospitals when they arrive.

I am sure that your brothers and other relatives enjoy receiving nice letters from you. When they return they undoubtedly will have wonderful stories to tell you.

The Chief Surgeon wishes me to thank you for your efforts in trying to make his patients happy.

Sincerely yours,

PAUL I. ROBINSON
Colonel, Medical Corps,
Deputy Chief Surgeon

As far as I can figure the letters in response to Betty's scrap book

began arriving in 1944, the first I fond was from Lieutenant H. R.

Anderson.

 April 4, 1944. That would make Betty 10 years old at that time.

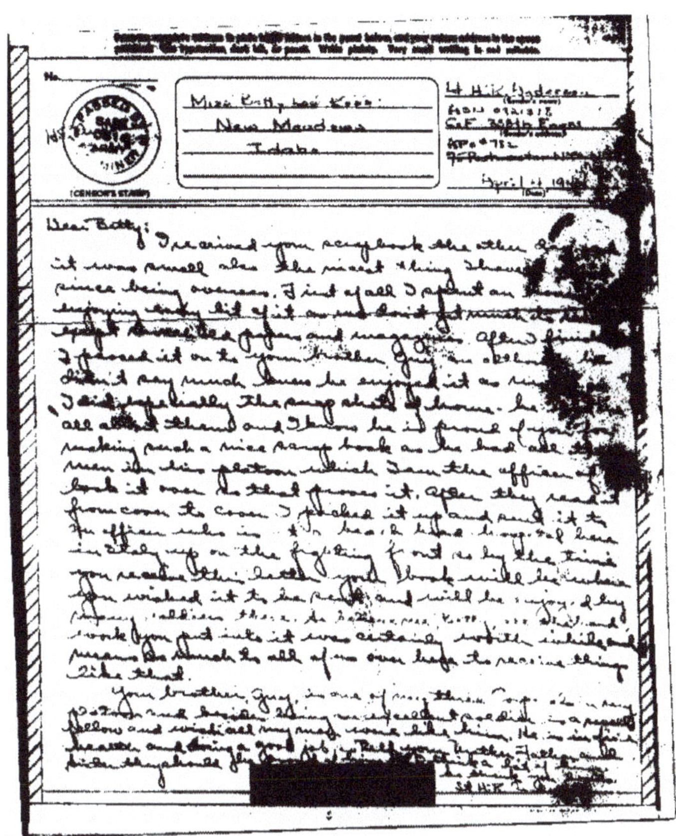

. Lieutenant H. R. Anderson   April 4, 1944

"I received your scrapbook the other day it was swell also the nicest thing I have (?) since being overseas. First of all I spent an hour enjoying every bit of it as we don't get much to read. I passed it on to your brother Guy and although he didn't say much know he enjoyed it as much as I did especially the snap shots of home. He told me all about them and I know he is proud of you for making such a nice scrap book as he had all the men from his platoon which I am the officer of look it over so that proves it. After they read it from cover to cover I packed it up and sent it to an officer at a beach head hospital here in Italy up on the fighting front so by the time you receive this letter your book will be where you wished it would be sent and will be enjoyed by many soldiers there. So believe me Betty all the hard work you put into it was certainly worth while and means so much to all of us over here to receive things like that.

Your brother Guy is one of my three Corporals in my platoon and besides being an excellent soldier is a swell fellow and wish all my men were like him. He is in fine health and doing a good job so tell your Mother, Father, and sister they should be proud of him as I think a lot of him. So thank you loads.

Sgt. H. R. Anderson"

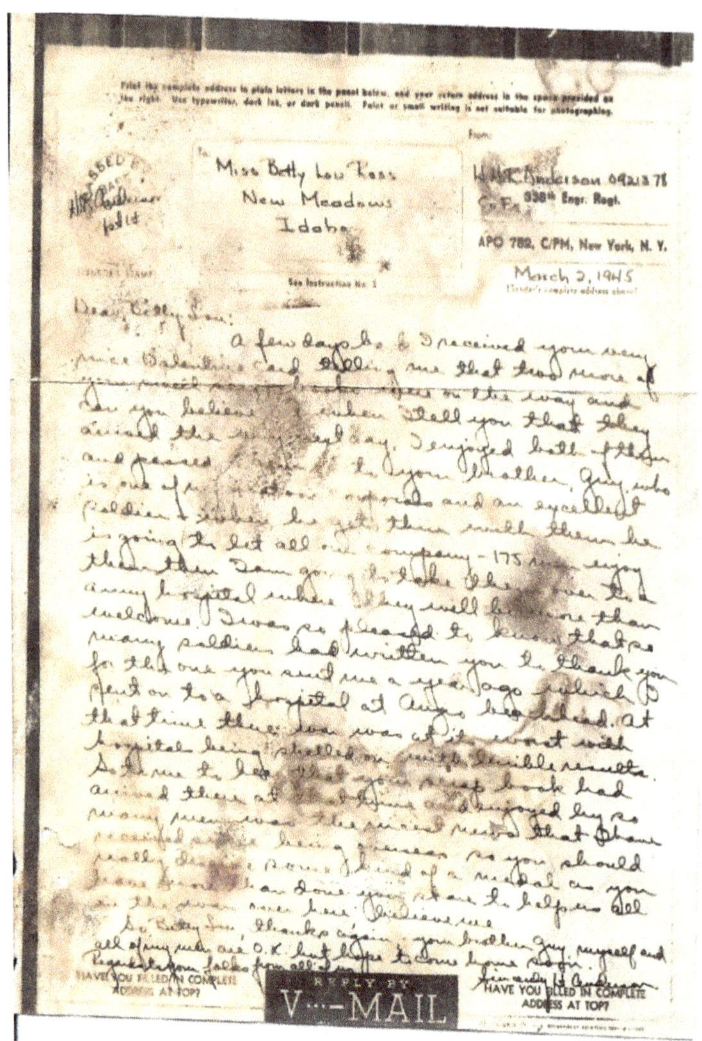

Lieutenant H. R. Anderson
0921378   338th Engr. Regt
March 2, 1945

Dear Betty Lou,

A few days back I received your very nice Valentine card telling me that two more of your swell scrap books were on the way and can you believe it when I tell you they arrived the very next day. I enjoyed both of them and passed them on to your brother Guy who is one of our platoon corporals and an excellent soldier …after? He get thru with them he is going to let all our company 175 enjoy them then I am going to take them over to an army hospital where they will be more than welcome. I was so pleased to know that so many soldiers had written you to thank you for the one you sent me a year ago which I sent on to a hospital at Arigio, beachhead. At that time the war was at its worst with hospitals being shelled on with terrible results. So to me to hear that your scrap books had arrived there at that time and enjoyed by so many …… the ….. news that I have received since being overseas. So you should really deserve some kind of medal as you have more than done your share to help us all in the war over here, believe me.

So Betty Lou, thanks again your brother Guy, myself and all my …. Are o.k. But hope to come home soon.

Regards to your folks from all of us.

Sincerely, H.R. Anderson

The Home Letter

BY L. M. THORNTON

Oh mighty mountain and restless sea,
  Oh shifting sands of the desert wide,
Be kind to the message that goes from
  me
    To the little home where my loved
      ones bide,
Be kind, nor halt it upon its track
O'er your winding ways, in the gray
    mail sack.

Oh white-winged vessel and rumbling
    train,
  Oh coach and horses that speed away,
My message bear through the sun and
    rain
    To the little home where my loved
      ones stay.
Nor praise, nor thanks shall you ever
    lack
For the prize you bring in the gray
    mail sack.

Oh night be loyal and day be kind;
  Oh winds be gentle, lest all too late
My tender message a transit find
    To the little home where my loved
      ones wait.
Forces unseen, make safe its track,
In the dark confines of the gray
    mail sack.

"12725, Greene Ave., Venice, Calif., March 28, 1945.

"Dear Miss Ross: I saw the article in The Leader this last week about the scrap books you are making for the service men. Recently when I was very ill, two little nieces sent these cartoons to me. They cut them out by their own selves and I thought it was very thoughtful of them. One is almost 8 and the other is 4. Since the cartoons gave me several good chuckles, and so much thoughtfulness was empodied in their gathering, I haven't wanted to destroy them. Consequently, when I saw the article in The Leader, I immediately knew what I would do with them. You will likely find a few that are not even funny, but most seemed good to me. I hope they help some service man to shed his war-weariness for a time. Good luck to you with your project. Sincerely, Mrs. Lawrence Cooper."

"P. S. We used to live at Council and are interested in the news from all around there, so we really enjoy our little paper. I used to work at the telephone office so a good many New Meadows names are familiar, although I've never seen the people."

This is the actual letter from Mrs. Lawrence Cooper march 28, 1945 as in the previous news article.

12725 Greene Ave.
Venice, Calif.
Mar. 29, 1945

Dear Miss Ross:

I saw the article in the [paper] last week about the scrap books you are making for the service men.

Recently when I was very ill two little nieces sent these cartoons to me. They cut them out by their own selves and I thought it was very thoughtful of them. One is almost 8 and the other is 4.

Since the cartoons gave me several good chuckles, and so much thoughtfulness was embodied in their gathering, I haven't wanted to destroy them. Consequently when I saw the [article] I immediately knew what I would do with them.

You will likely find a few that aren't them very funny but they all look good to me. I hope they will some service man to shed his war-weariness for a time.

I am [sending] back to you with your [scrapbook].

Sincerely

Mrs. Lawrence Cooper

P.S. We used to live at Council and are very interested in the news from all around there so we really enjoy our little paper. I did to work in the telephone office so [many] New Meadows names are somewhat like I've never seen the people.

62

**Mrs. John Mitchell
April 7, 1945**

Dear Betty Lou,

I read in yesterday morning's Spokesman Review a nice article saying you write to hundreds of service men as per pen pals. I write to service men as pen pals too. I have been trying to get more addresses of service men and was wondering if you would send me a list of names of some of your pals so I could write to some of them too.

Would be glad to correspond with you too if you care to. Please answer right away and <u>please</u> fill my heart's desire by

sending me some of the boys addresses. I will appreciate it very much. I write letters as one of my hobbies. Well will close hoping to hear from you real____ <u>soon</u>, till then

I remain a friend

Mrs. John Mitchell

Tekoa, Wash.   Box 168

P.S. A very good soldier pen pal of mine would like some more pen pals. His address is: Pvt. Charles Elder A.S.N. 34793497 Sec. Q Bks 250 3505th A.A.F. Base   Unit Scott Field, Illinois He writes very nice letter. He is married.

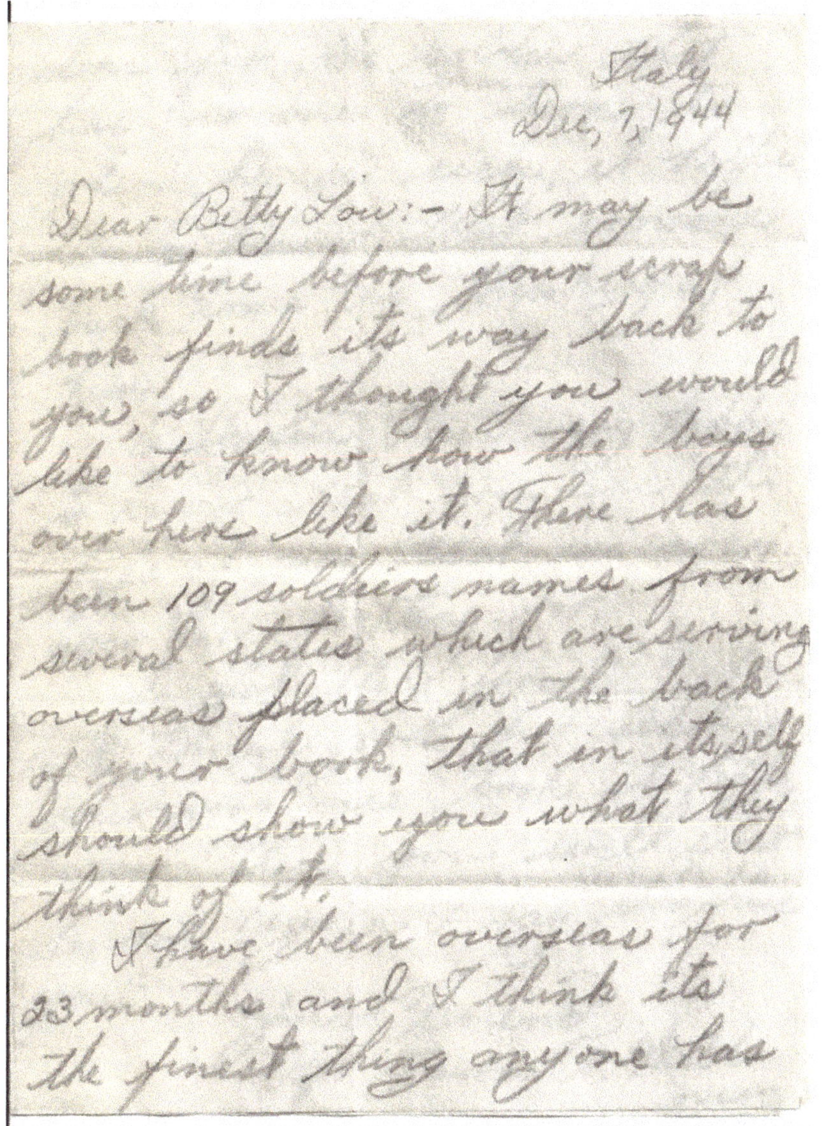

PFC James Webb
Dec. 7, 1944
Italy

Dear Betty Lou:- It may be some time before your scrap book finds its way back to you, so I thought you would like to know how the boys over here like it. There has been 109 soldiers names from several states which are serving overseas placed in the back of your book, that in itself should show you what they think of it.

I have been overseas for 23 months and I think it's the finest thing anyone has

Page 2

Done for the soldier that has no one to turn to when he is sick, it helps him to know that someone back home is thinking of him.

Betty Lou, I am very happy to know that you are the type of girl that we are over here fighting for.

So God bless you Betty Lou and thank you for sending your very nice book it helps more than you will ever know. Again I say "God bless you"

Your Friend

Pfc. James F. Webb

over

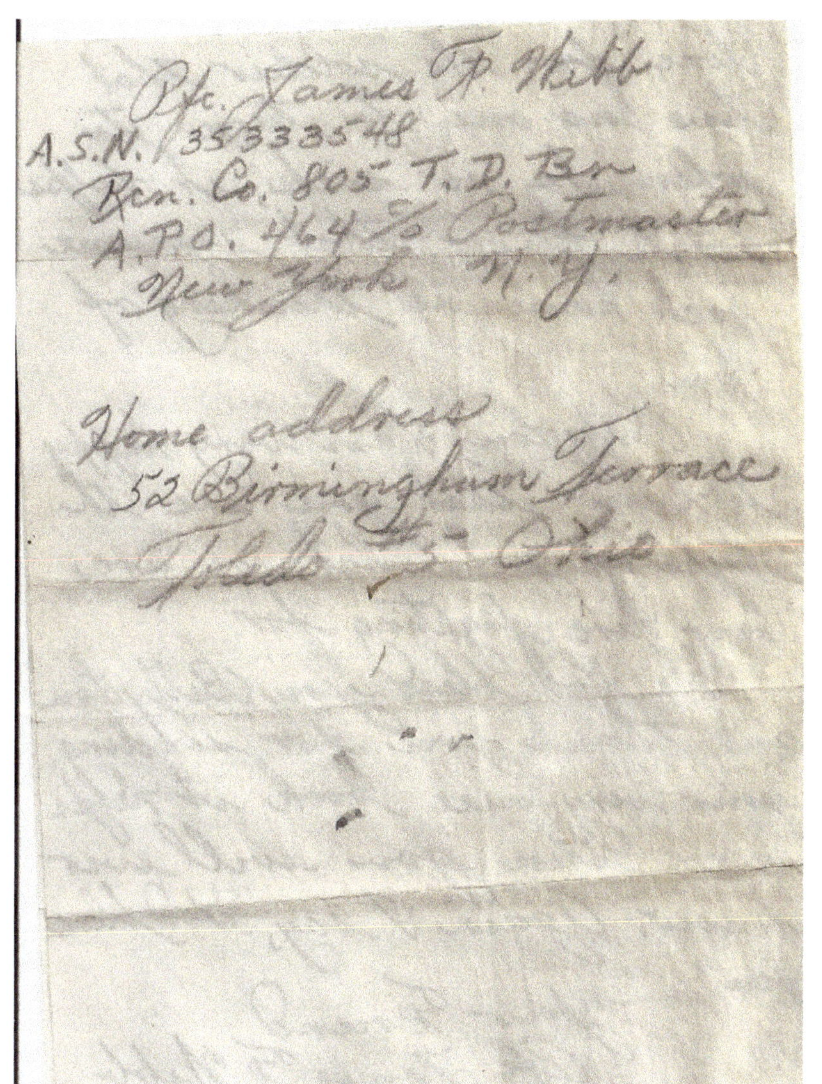

PFC James Webb
Dec. 7, 1944 Italy

Page 3
Pfc. James F. Webb
A.S.N.35333548
Rcn. Co. 805 T.D. Bn
A.P.O. 464 c/o
Postmaster
New York N.Y.

Home address
52 Birmingham Terrace
Toledo #5 Ohio

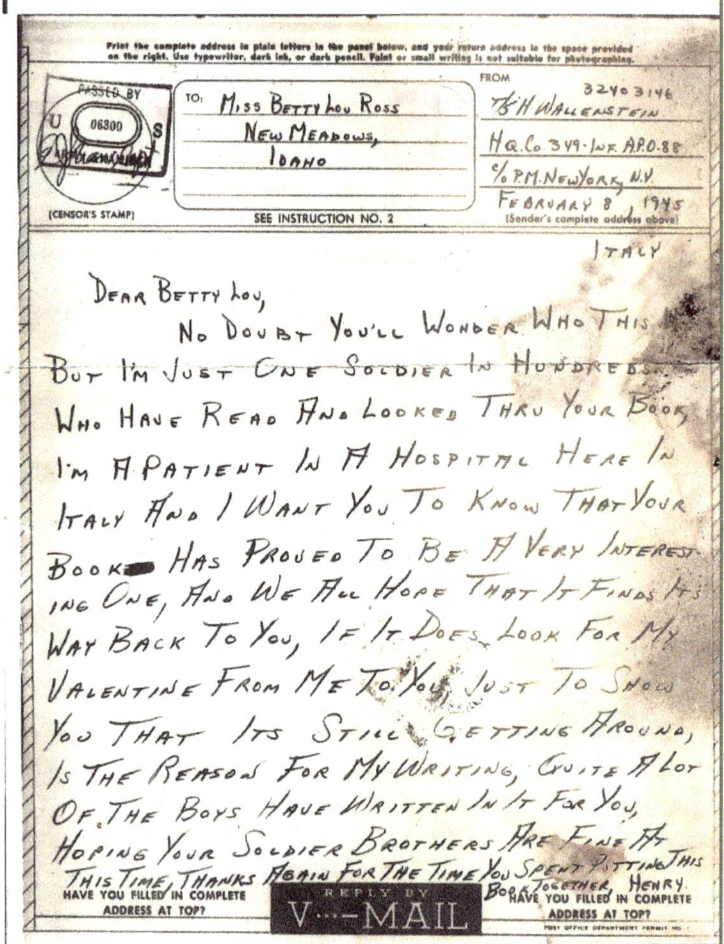

Henry Wallenstein
Feb. 8, 1945 Italy

Dear Betty Lou

No doubt you'll wonder who this is but I'm just one soldier in hundreds who have read and looked thru your book, I'm a patient in a hospital here in Italy and I want you to know your book has proved to be a very interesting one, and we all hope that it finds its way back to you, if it does look for my Valentine from me to you, just to show you that its still getting around, is the reason for my writing, quite a lot of the boys have written in it for you, Hoping your soldier brothers are fine at this time, Thanks again for the time you spent putting this book together, Henry

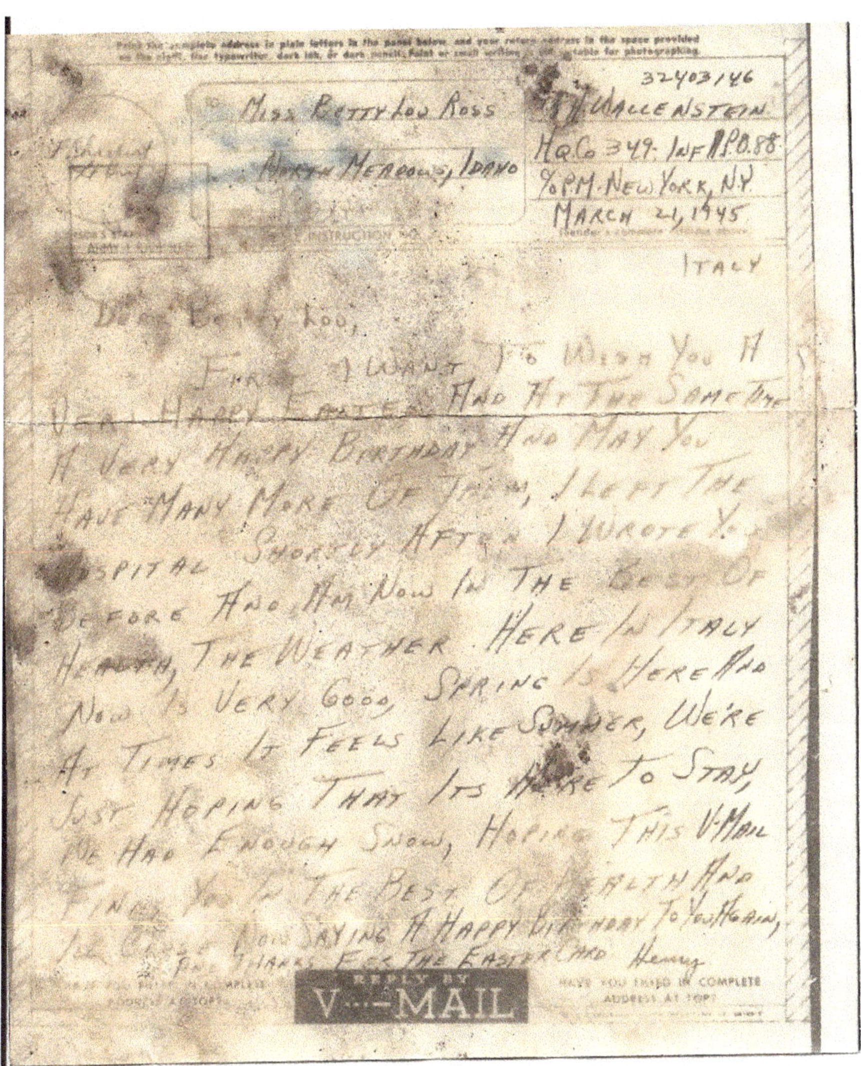

Henry Wallenstein
March 21, 1945
Italy

Dear Betty Lou,

First I want to wish you a very Happy Easter and at the same time a very Happy Birthday and may you have many more of them, I left the hospital shortly after I wrote you before and am now in the best of health, the weather here in Italy now is very good, Spring is here and at times it feels like Summer, we'er just hoping that its here to stay, We had enough snow, hoping this V-Mail finds you in the best of health and will close now saying a Happy Birthday to you again, and thanks for the Easter card

Henry

Henry Wallenstein
Aug.24, 1945
Verona, Italy

Dear Betty Lou,

I'm sorry I haven't answered you letter sooner, and thank you for the picture of yourself and your two brothers, Im enclosing a couple of snapshots of myself taken in Merano, Italy, that's up near the Austrian border.

One is taken on my day off, and the other I'm supposed to be working, but at that moment I'm resting, in our Motor pool, that's not jeep, im just sitting in it, and that's a little Italian girl about the same age as yourself, So long for now Betty Lou.

Your Friend, Henry,

This letter was addressed to Betty Lou

In salutations he writes Mary Lou.

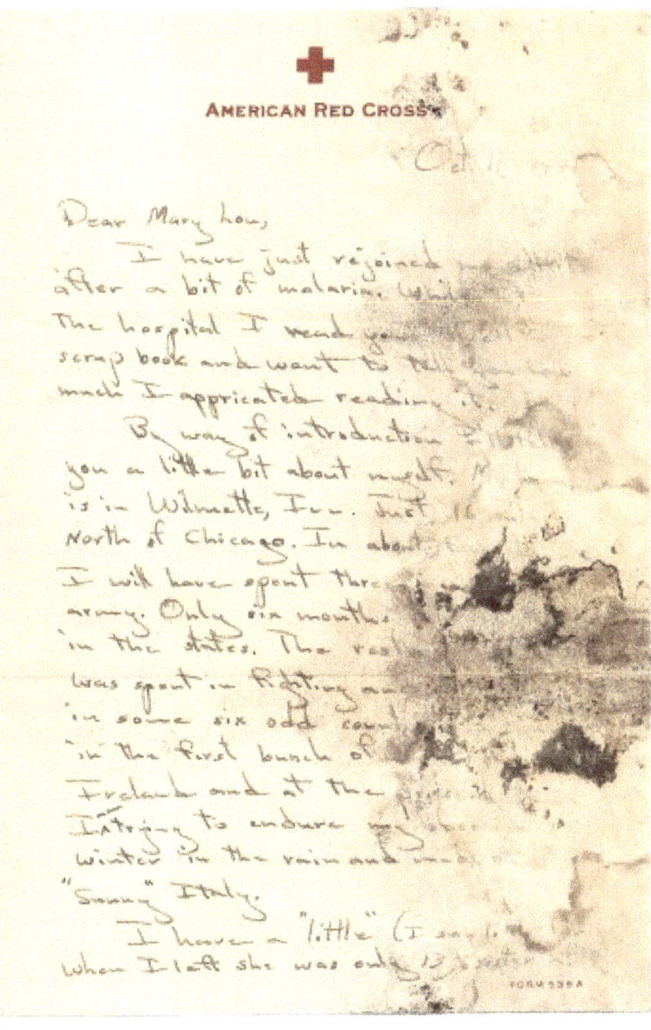

James R. Edwards HQ Co.
701st T.D. APO 464, c/o N.C.C.
Oct. 11, 1944

Dear Mary Lou,

I have just rejoined my outfit after a bit of malaria. While in the hospital I read your well …scrap book and wanted to tell you how much I appreciated reading it.

By the way of introduction I will tell you a little bit about myself. My home is in Wilmette, Ill. Just 16 miles north of Chicago. In about four ….I will have spent three …… army. Only six months….in the states. The rest ……was spent fighting and ….in some six odd countries…In the first bunch of…..Ireland and at the ….

I am trying to endure my second winter in the rain and mud of "sunny" Italy.

I have a "little" (I say little for when I left she was only 13, sister at

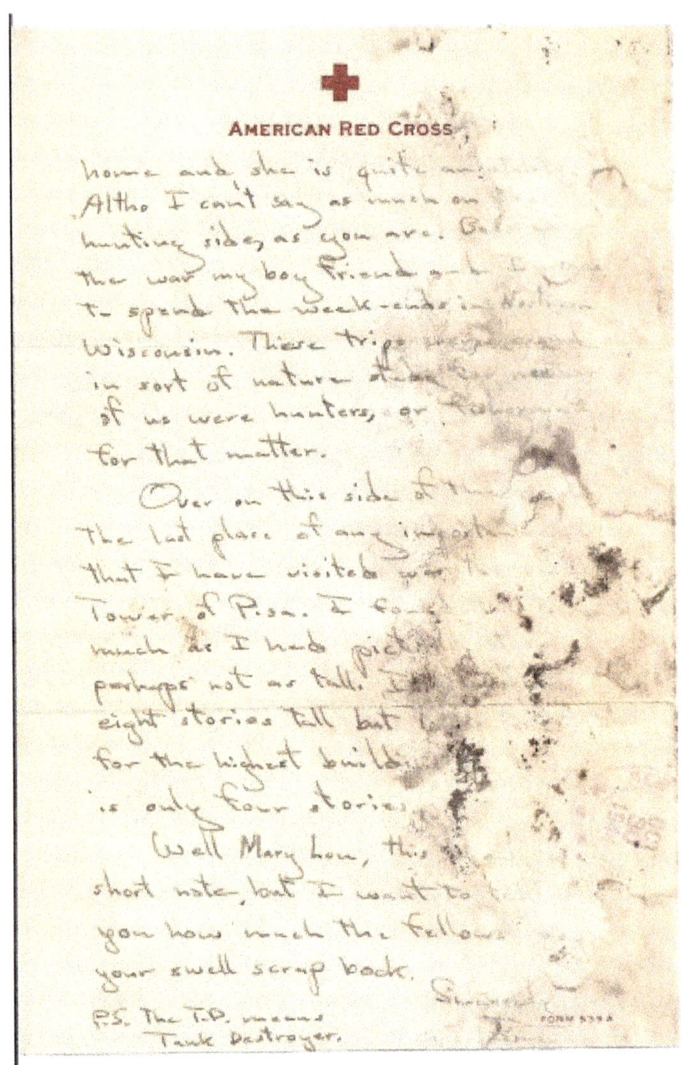

James R. Edwards HQ Co. 701st T.D. APO 464, c/o N.C.C. Oct. 11, 1944

Page 2

Home she is quite an athlete.

Altho I can't say as much on the ….hunting side as you are. Before the war my boy friend and I used to spend the weekends in Northern Wisconsin. These trips were spent in sort of nature studies, for neither of us were hunters, or fishermen for that matter.

Over on this side of the pond the last place of any importance was the Tower of Pisa. I found….much as I had picture….perhaps not as tall. I'll….eight stories tall but I…..for the highest building….is only four stories.

Well Mary Lou this is a short note, but I want to tell you how much the fellows enjoy your swell scrap book.

Sincerely Jim

PS The T.D. means

Tank Destroyer

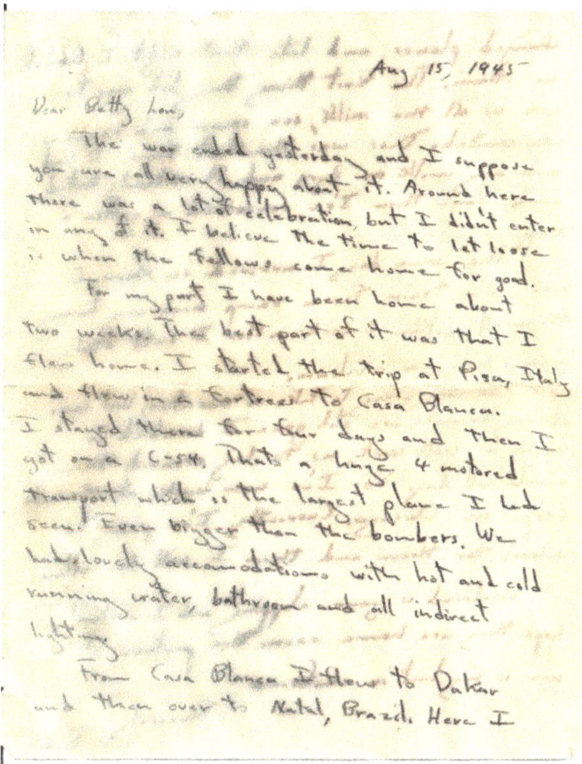

James Edwards
Aug. 15, 1945

Page 1

Dear Betty Lou,

The war ended yesterday and I suppose you are all very happy about it. Around here there was a lot of celebration, but I didn't enter in any of it. I believe the time to let loose is when the fellows come home for good.

For my part I have been home about two weeks. The best part of it was that I flew home. I started the trip at Pisa, Italy and flew in a fortrees(?) to Casa Blanca.

I stayed there for four days and then I got on a C-54 that's a huge 4 motored transport which is the largest plane I had seen. Even bigger than the bombers, We had lovely accomodations with hot and cold water, bathroom and all indirect lighting.

From Casa Blanca I flew to Dakar and then over to Natal, Brazil. Here I

Page 2

Changed planes and late that night I landed in Miami. The first thing they did was to give us all the milk, ice cream and bananas we wanted. This was the first time I had had any milk in 3 yrs. And it certainly tasted good. Since then I've consumed a gallon a day.

The same day I arrived in Miami, I was on a train for a camp near my home. All in all within 2 weeks after I left Italy I was home a civilian.

I was going to take a vacation, but since all my friends are still gone I decided I might as well work, as to lay around the beach all day. So I'm now back at Masonite Corp. in Chicago. Currently I'm going to school for them and then I will be selling.

Enclosed is your clipping and I certainly hope you are home soon. The picture of me is my last in uniform.

Sincerely, Jim

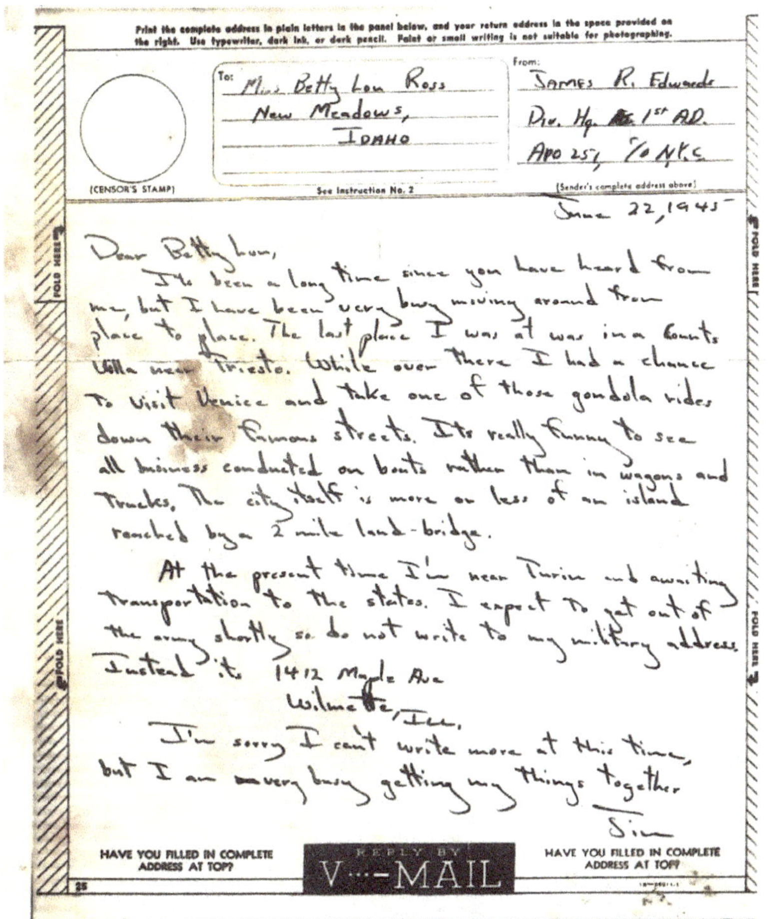

James R. Edwards
June 22, 1945

Dear Betty Lou,

It's been a long time since you have heard from me, but I have been very busy moving around from place to place. The last place I was at was in a Counts Villa near Trieste. While over there I had a chance to visit Venice and take one of those gondola rides down their famous streets. Its really funny to see all business conducted on boats rather than in wagons and trucks. The city itself is more or less an island reached by a 2 mile land-bridge.

At the present time I'm near Turin(?) and awaiting transportation to the states. I expect to get out of the army shortly so do not write to my military address.

Instead its.

1412 Maple Ave

Wilmette/ Ill.

I'm sorry I can't write more at this time, but I am very busy getting things together.

Jim

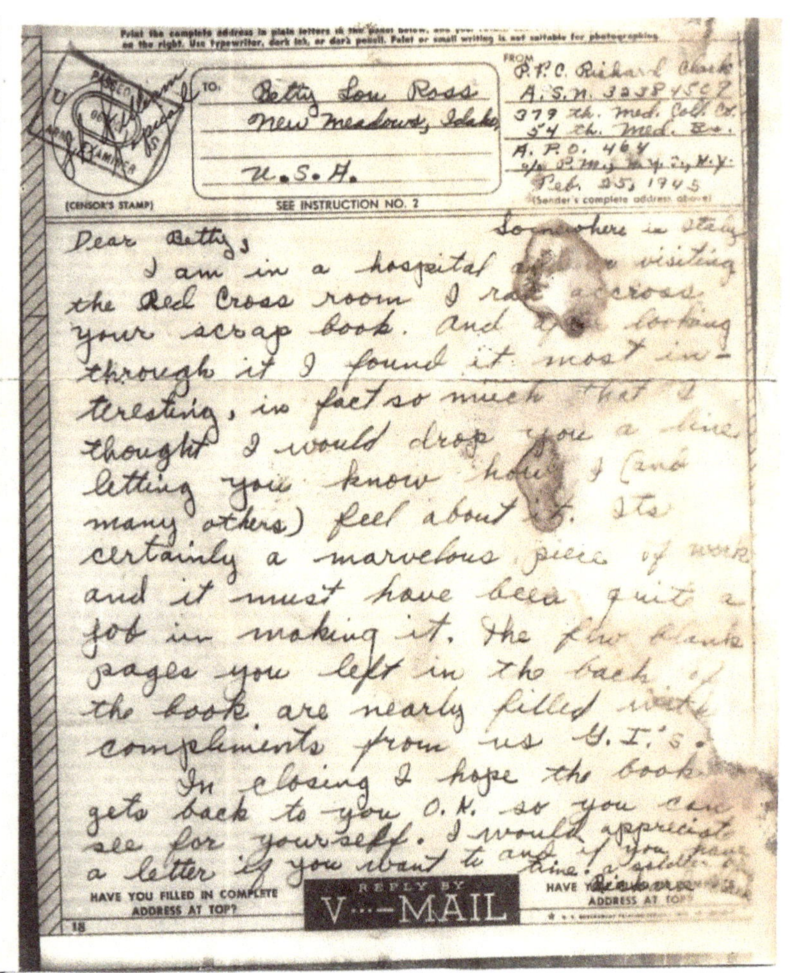

P.F.C. Richard Clark

A.S.N. 32384509 379th Med Coll. CO. 54th Med Bs. A.P.O. 464

Feb.25, 1945

Somewhere in Italy

Dear Betty,

I am in a hospital and are visiting the Red Cross room I ran across your scrap book. And after looking through it I found it most interesting., in fact so much that I thought I would drop you a line letting you know I (and many ohers) feel about it. Its certainly a marvelous piece of work and it must have been quite a job making it. The first blank pages you left in the back of the book are nearly filled with compliments from us G.I.'s.

In closing I hope the book gets back to you o.k. so you can see for yourself. I would appreciate a letter if you want to and if you have the time.

A Soldier

Richard

Richard Clark
May 16, 1945

Dear Betty Lou,

Just received your most welcomed letter with the snap shot and thanks a lot.

Am enclosing a picture post card of the beautiful scenery we have here in the Alps Mnt. Of course this isn't so much snow now but its still very beautiful with all the snow capped mt. peaks and green valleys.

When I get a snap shot of myself I will send you one. You are a very cute kid- I hope you don't mind me saying so. All my buddies say it

S. Martino De Castrozza Austria May 16, 1945

Page 2

When I show your snap shot to them.

Well Betty, I will try to answer your questions. My home is in Syracuse, N.Y. That's in the central part of the N.Y. State. I only have one brother and he's older than me and in the army in Europe somewhere. He's married and has a son about 2 yrs. Old.

Yes, I'm out of the hospital now and feeling fine. It sure feels good to have the war over with. The cities are all lit up at night. The first we've seen for over two years.

Well Betty, I will close for now hoping to hear from you again.

A friend Richard

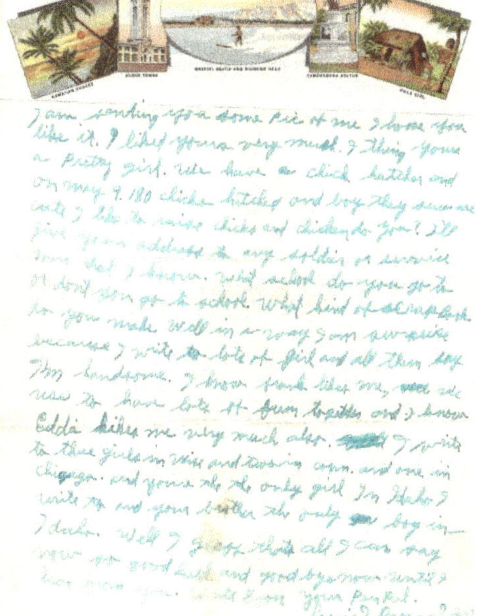

Louis Paraga
May 15, 1945
Kekaha Kauai

Dear Betty Lou,

Received your most expected letter today. I will be very glad to correspond with you so don't worry about my answering your letters. I hope you are fine for myself I am in the best of health. I received a letter of the Marine yesterday and answered it right away and so I didn't know I'd received your letter today. Thanks very much for sending me that news paper clip about you. You must be a very popular girl in your town are you? I have 3 sisters and two brother my oldest sister is married to a civilian boy her name is Mildred the comes Mary that's the pic of her I sent your bro. she is going to be 19 then comes me Louis I am going to be 18 Oct. 31 Then comes Anton...........

Louis Paraga   May 15, 1945   Kekaha Kauai

I am sending you some pic of me I hope you like it I like your very much. I thing youre a pretty girl. We have a chick hatcher and on May 9. 180 chicks hatched and boy they sure are cute I like to raise chicks and chickens do you? I'll give your address to any soldier or service men that I know. What school do you go to or don't you go to school. What kind of scrap book do you make. Well in a way I am surprise because I write to lots of girl and all them say I am handsome. I know frank likes me we used to have lots of fun together and I know Eddie like me very much also. I write to three girls in Wis. And two in Conn. And one in Chicago. And youre the only girl I write to in Idaho and your brother the only boy in Idaho. Well I guess that's all I can say now so good luck and good bye now until I hear from you. Write soon your pen pal

Louis Paraga Jr.

One of the Soldiers sent this napkin that was in her scrap book.

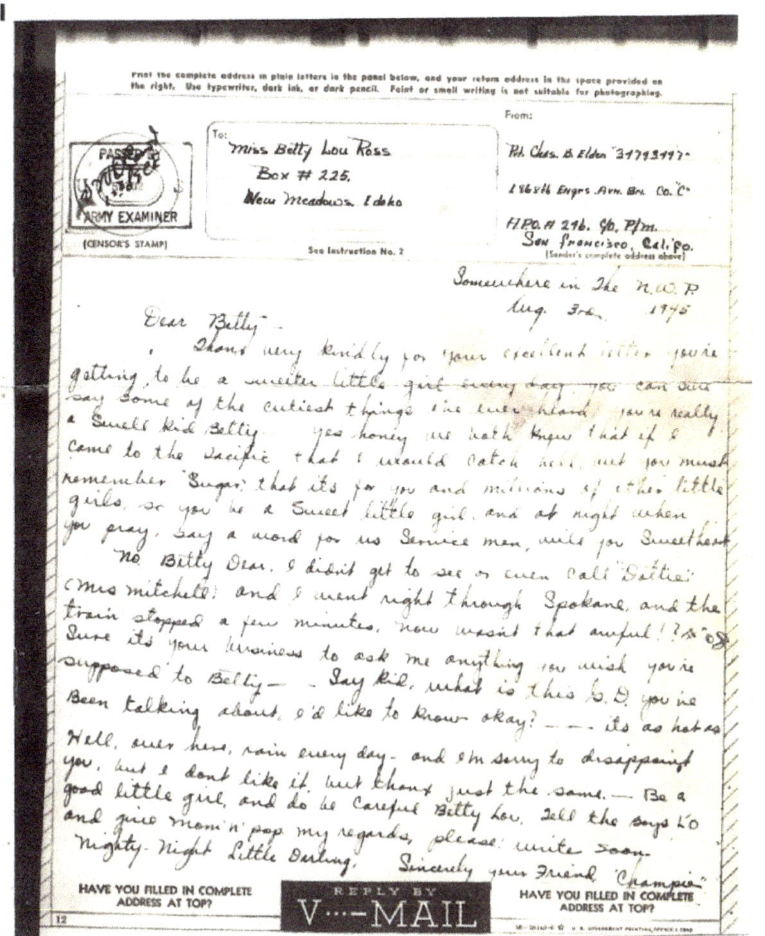

Dear Betty,

Thankx very kindly for your excellent letter you're getting to be a sweeter little girl every day you can sure say some of the cutest things I've ever heard you're really a swell kid Betty. Yes honey we both knew that if I came to the Pacific that I would catch hell. And you must remember "sugar" that it's for you and millions of other little girls. So you be a sweet little girl, and at night when you pray, say a word for us service men, will you sweetheart.

No Betty Dear, I didn't get to see or even call "Dottie" (Mrs. Mitchell) and I went right through Spokane, and the train stopped a few minutes, now wasn't that awful!?#o8.

Sure it's your business to ask me anything you wish you're supposed to Betty. Say kid what is this G.D. you've been talking about I'd like to know- ok? Its as bad as Hell, over here, rain every day-I'm sorry to disappoint you, but I don't like it, but thanx just the same. Be a good little gir,l and do be careful Betty Lou. Tell the boys L'o and give Mom 'n' pop my regards, please. Write soon.

Nighty-Night Little Darling

Sincerely your friend,

"Champie"

Dearest Betty,

Thnax so much for such a lovely letter I think you're such a swell kid- Hope all are happy now that you say the war is over- careful and don't over sport yourself and don't try to get all the shall I say victory kisses (smile), no doubt you're over stocked with em' now already-remember there's still quite a few of us fellows left over here yet, and we are expecting kisses to when we return have you any more left? I don't see how you can possible have- do you?

Sure! Betty Honey, you do have a number of things to be very, very proud of, and I am awful proud of you too so you can add my name to your g.d. list with "thanx so much" and really I don't know how to tell you just how grateful I am for the grand compliments you've given me- I think you're wonderful! Betty Lou- so you've placed me on your Special List. Huh! That's very sweet of you kid- you know Betty sometimes I don't know how to figure you out- you're you but you are so Brilliant, and say the sweetest things at times, and besides you're very smart "at times" cry a little tho (ha' ha')

Say Betty what do you mean I'll do you like I did Mrs. Mitchell Something bad? Are you seeing many good movies nowadays? I'm not- Well "precious" I guess this is all for now. So be a good little girl, and take good care of yourself- give my regards to your family and write soon you've been very faithful so far and awful nice about everything. Thanx again for the grand letter.

Sincerely yours,

"Champ"

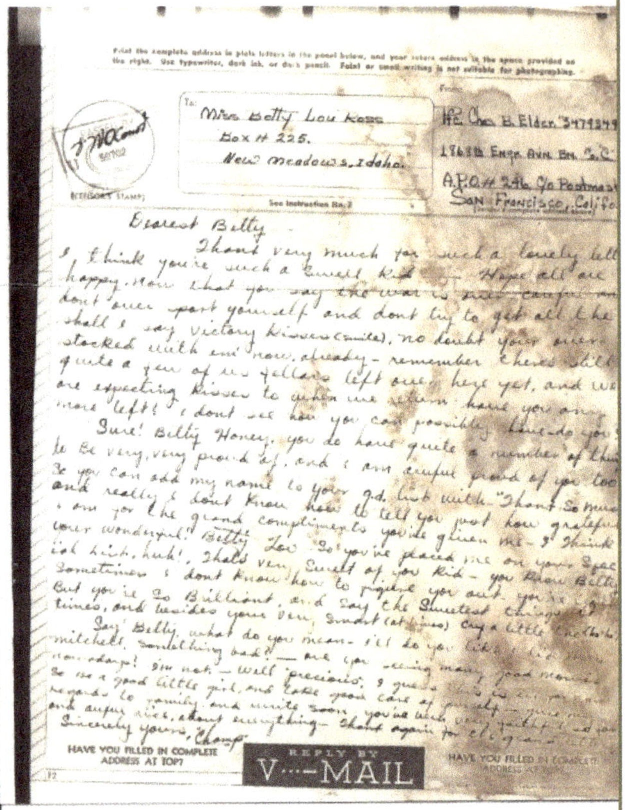

Chas Elder Greenville Air Base May 27, 1945

Dear Betty-

Rc'd your grand letter dated the 8th just today due to the fact that I've just came back off 21 days Furlo- No doubt you've said I was not a real Pal But now you know why it's taken so long for you to receive an answer right….right(?)

I am very glad to add you to my very long list of pals and friends, And thanx………and the pictures are wonderful…..awful cute Betty… the grandest parents….. to be so very nice yourself.

Know you're very………

Thanx very kindly for the……about the….But

Chas Elder Greenville Air Base May 27, 1945

Page 2

This first part of the second page is not legible, I can only make out a few words, until further down. I will write the words I can make out.

Still….the same…..it…me feel good to….like you feel…..boys fighting…….but I don't mind…. have two Bros. over and……..There's 6 of us…….last one to go, or come in rather……..

Betty Honey I'm awful sorry but I can't keep a snap shot for a minute. So if you wont be mad at me… s one as soon as I have some more made, ok? By the way kid how old are you, Please? And what does G.D. Album mean? (smile) don't be afraid to say anything you want to me, because I've heard practically everything I S'pose.

Ask any question you wish. Give family my regards ans. At once, please!

Adios Senorita Ross,

Love Chas

My Dear Betty Lou,

I don't know how to begin to thank for the joy & happiness these pictures & the jokes you sent in the scrap books. There are 2 of them here, in the hospital in Manila. I'm in here as a patient with fallen arches & Arthritus, & can't hardly get around. Down in the lobby, (we'll call'it) of this blding there's tables & chairs to rite & also a book case of books. There are papers & magazines or other stands & your scrap books, which I hated to open at first, perticulary the one with a picture of a baby & a soldier together. It brought tears to my eyes, but I enjoyed it. It brought back mimories of my wife & son home waiting for my return, which I hope is soon. Betty Lou, I want to thank you for doing more than your share in the war effort. & I thank the Lord Jesus Crist

2.

Pg 2

For bringing into the world a baby girl who must understand the Longing & Suffering a soldier goes throughwhile he is waiting & waiting to go home to his loved ones.

Betty I feel like a brother to you or something as that. You are an angle sent from God to cheer the hearts of men.
May God Bless & Protect you Betty, for the Lord must have a mission for you to perform in this World.
May God be with you & I thank you from the bottom of my heart.
To an angle Betty Lou
From a Happy Soldier,
Johnny

P.F.C. John P. Ruth Jr. 36...717
3017 omaco 141 OBA M.BN
A.P.O. 75
P.M. SAN FRANCISCO, CALIF

Dear Betty,
Received your letter the other day and was very glad to hear from you. I'm in school and haven't anything to do.

Glad to hear your leg is better. How is everything else? Everyone here ok all except we have colds. We sure are having nasty weather one day warm next day raining and the next it's snowing . The last week it has been mostly raining and snowing.
Last Saturday nite I had a birthday party on my girl friend and all these guys came over and crashed it well the kids that were invited left and after they did boy did the boys & I have it round and round. This Rick that

I used to go with we argued and argued gee whiz we even dug up things as far back as last August.
We were alone for about 1 hour & had plenty of time to do it in too before the others came back.
Guess I better close for now and I will write more later as I just remembered I have Economics to do.
Marilyn

P.S. Sorry I can't think of any more to write but at least I am answering. I guess I told you about my niece if I didn't I'm sure I'm slipping & she was 3 months old last Friday she sure is getting sweet. I haven't been able to see her for almost 2 weeks because of my cold. Went to a dance last Friday with Roy & was coughing so we couldn't dance Some fun.
Will close for sure

On the side
Have you heard from Belvin? I haven't

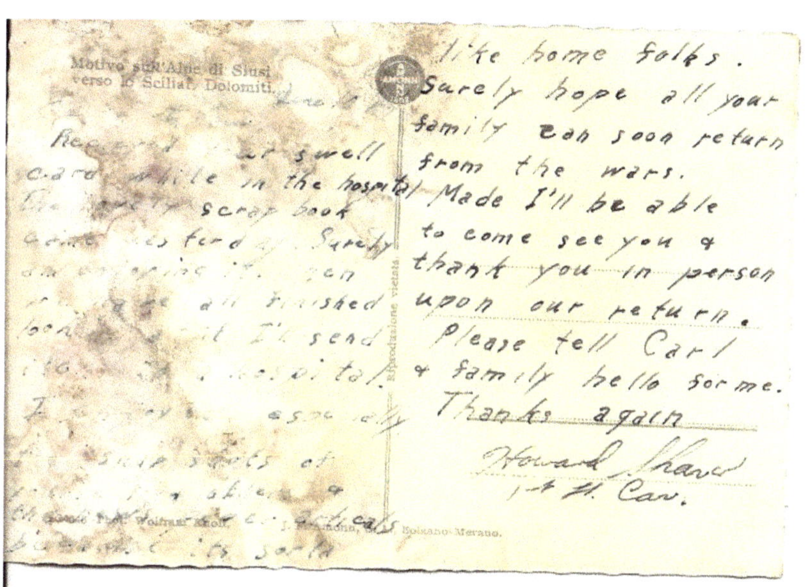

Howard Shaver
June 11, 1945

Dear Betty Lou,

Received your swell card while in the hospital The heavenly scrap book came this Friday Surly am enjoying it. When we are all finished looking at it I 'll send it to a hospital.

I enjoy …. especially the snapshot of yourself and others and the news paper articles because its sorta like home folks.

Surely hope all your family can soon return from the wars.

Made I'll be able to come see you and thank you in person upon our return.

Please tell Carl and family hello from me.

Thanks again

Howard Shaver

1st Lt. Cav.

Many soldiers wrote to Betty but one of the most often was Belvin Kroger. Belvin "Bill" had a niece that lived in Flint, Michigan by the name of Marilyn Melacon. Marilyn became a pen pal as well to Betty.

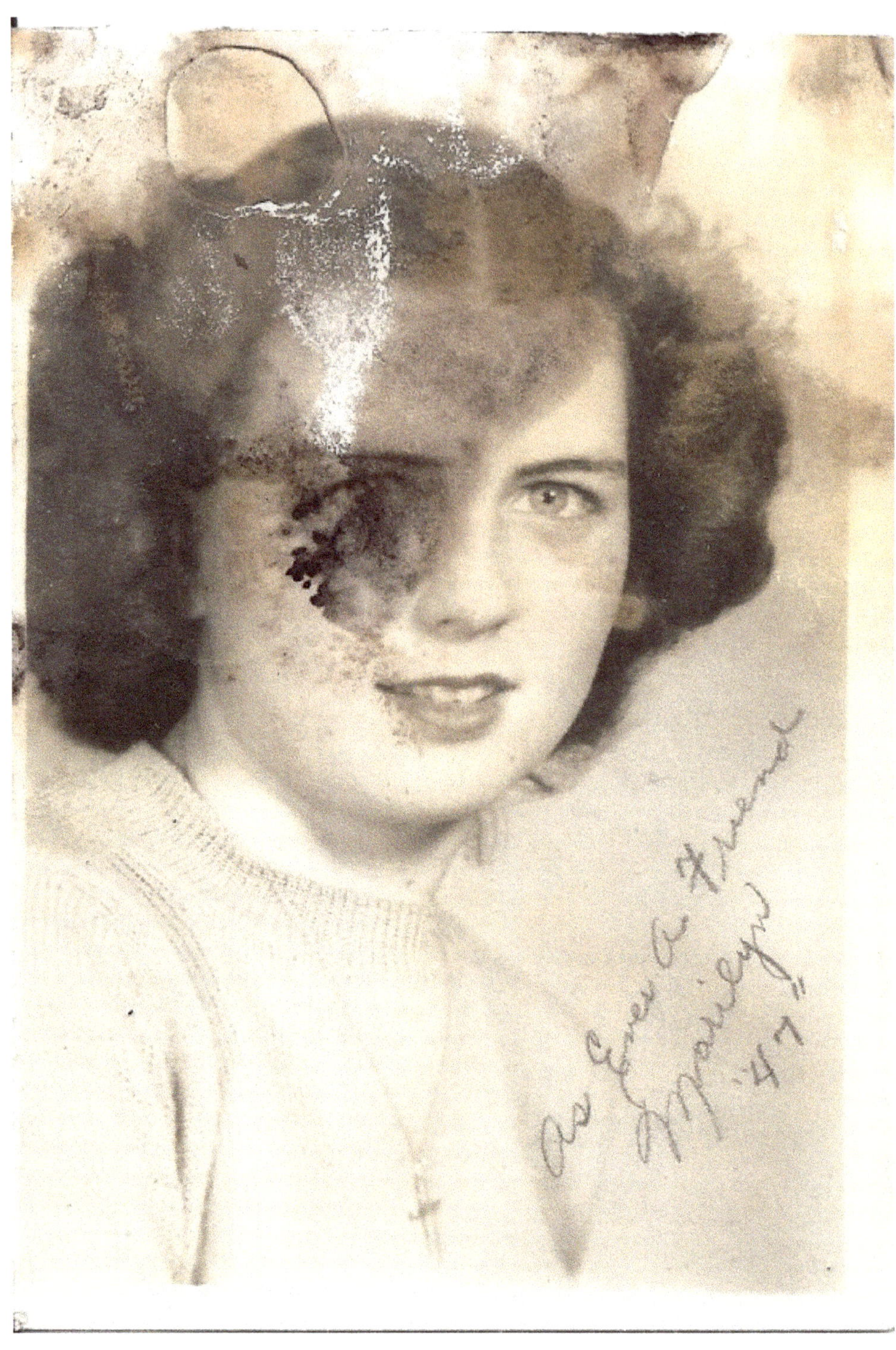

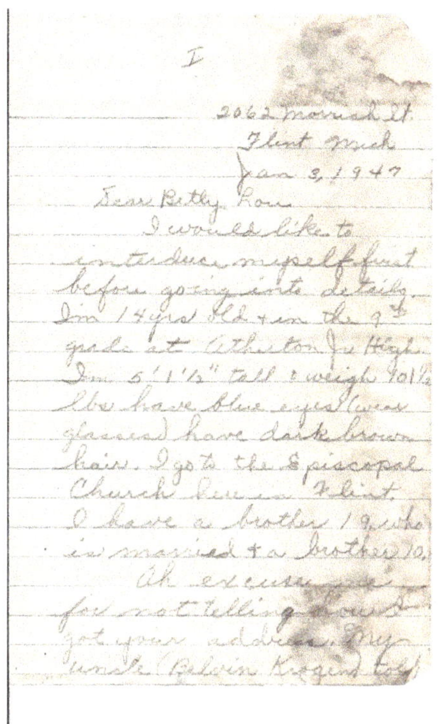

2062 Moorish St.

Flint MI

January 3rd, 1947

Dear Betty Lou,

I would like to introduce myself first before going into details I'm 14 years old and I'm the 9th grade at Atherton Jr High I'm 5 foot 1 1/2 inch tall and weigh 101 1/2 pounds have blue eyes and wear glasses have dark brown hair I go to the Episcopal Church here in Flint. I have a brother 19 who is married and a brother 10 oh excuse me for not telling how I got your address my uncle Belvin Kroger told

me about you and sent me your address and asked me to write to you he said I would find you very interesting. And he also would like to know why you haven't written in case you have lost his address here it is Belvin O. Kroger 415 Bernville St. New Orleans LA.

He also would like to know how you're getting along I hope you will excuse such a small letter and all because I'm not much of a hand at writing uh to new people the first time but

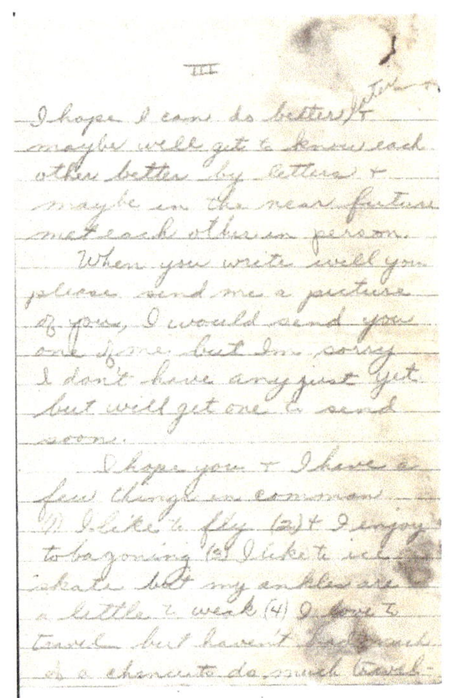

I hope I can do better later & maybe well get to know each other better by letters & maybe in the near future met each other in person.

When you write will you please send me a picture of you, I would send you one of me but Im sorry I don't have any just yet but will get one send soon.

I hope you and I have a few things in common one I like to fly two I enjoy tobogganing 3 I like to ice skate but my ankles are a little too weak four I love to travel but haven't had much of a chance to do much travel

Ing But I have been in this states Ohio, Ill, Ind. & Mich of course.

I don't enjoy base ball & such as that ony to go & oldwatch. In the summer I like to take long walks in the woods, & swim if I knew how. I love to work around flowers also & I just love cats I have one he is dark brown & sort of light in spots has a white chest & he has just a little of white on his fwwt he is 17 wks old & is as small as he was when I got him when he was 5 wks old maybe a little bigger but not much. My sister-in-law

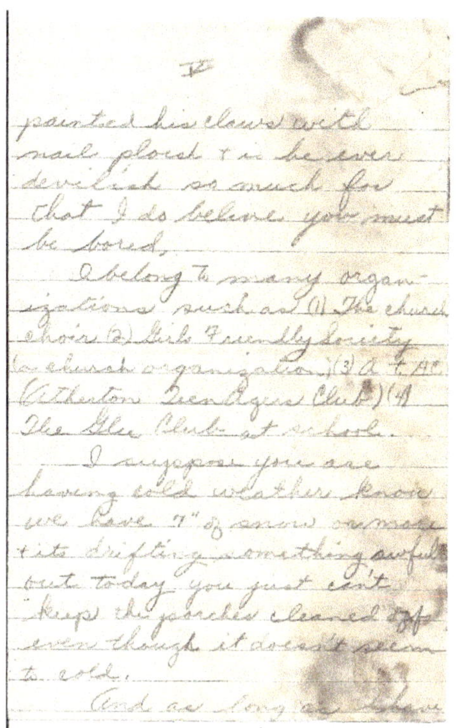

Painted his claws with nail polish & is he ever devilish so much for that I do believe you must be bored, I belong to many Organizations such as (1) The church choir (2) Girls Friendly Society (a church organization) (3) A.T.A.C. (Atherton Teenagers Club) (4) The Glee Club at school. I suppose you are having cold weather know we have 7" of snow or more & its drifting something awful out today you just can't keep the porches cleaned off even though it doesn't seem cold. And as long as I have

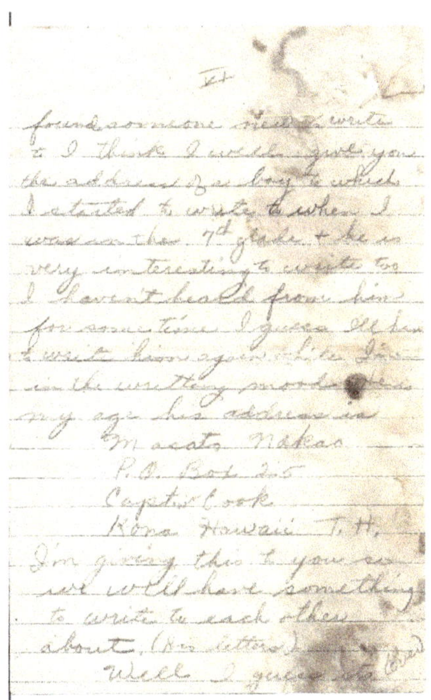

Found someone new to write to I think I will give you the address of a boy to which I started to write to when I was in the 7th grade & he is very interesting to write too I haven't heard from him for some time I guess I'll have to write him again while I'm in the writing mood He is my age his address is

Masato Nakas

P.O. Box 25

Captain Cook

Kona Hawaii T. H.

I'm giving this to you so we will have something to write each other about (his letters)

Well I guess its (Over)

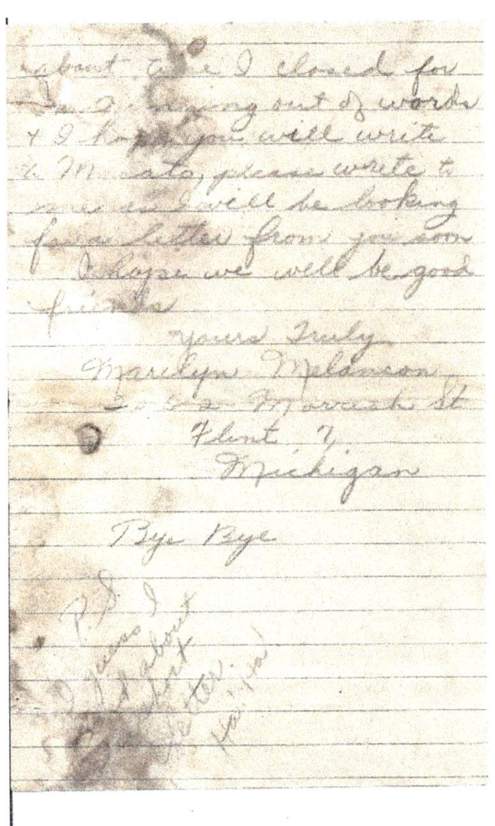

About time I close for Im running out of words & I hope you will write to Masato, please write to me as I will be looking for a letter from you soon I hope we will be good friends

Yours Truly

Marilyn Melancon

2062 Morrish St.

Flint 7,

Michigan

Bye Bye

P.S.

I guess I Lied about a short Letter Ha! Ha!

2062 Morrish Street

Flint Mich.

Jan. 30 1947

Dear Betty Lou,

Rec'd your letter last week but haven't had time to answer it yet so hope I'm excused. Thanks for the picture of yourself, I'll send you one of my school pictures when they come.

You mentioned having two brothers in the hospital, & I was wondering what was wrong if you care to tell. Say could you get some other girls or boys to write me & I'll try & do the same for you. Please because I love to correspond to people in other states I learn more that way & I'm sure you'd enjoy it too.

Say did you write to my Uncle Belvin
yet.

Gee I hope next time you write me you
ask me a lot of questions because I
don't know of anything to write just
know.

So guess I'll close.

As Ever Your Friend

Marilyn Melancon

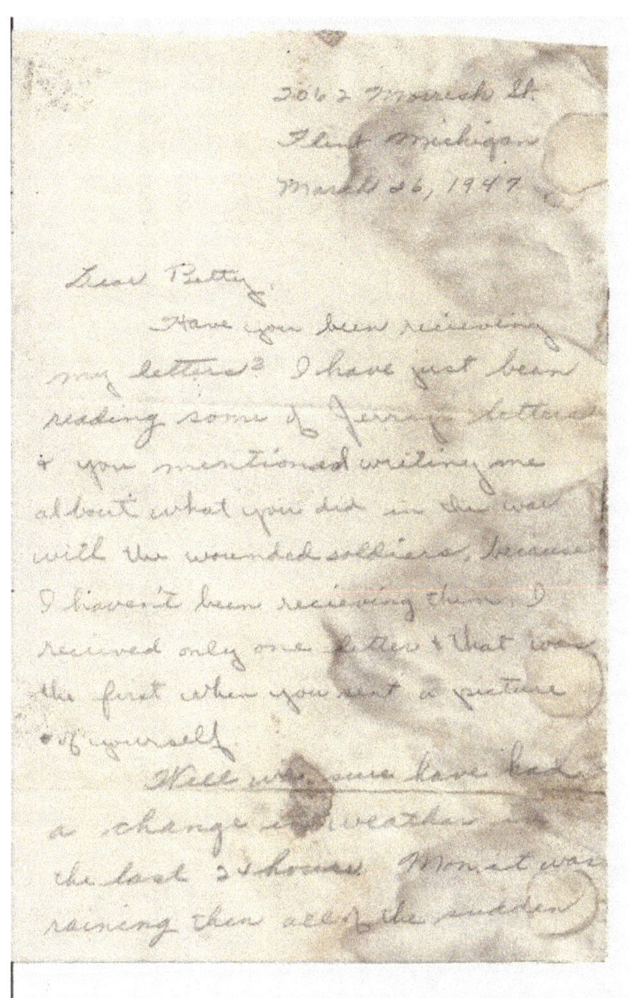

*2062 Morrich St
Flint Michigan
March 26, 1947
Dear Betty,
Have you been receiving my letters? I have just been reading some of Jerrys letters & you mentioned writing me albout what you did in the war with the wounded soldiers, because I haven't been receiving them. I received only one letter & that was the first when you sent a picture of yourself.
Well we sure have had a change in weather in the last 24 hours. Mon it was raining then all of the sudden*

2062 Morrish St
Flint, Michigan
4-14-49

Dear Betty,
Excuse the pecil because I'm in school.
My dad had his operation this morning at 8:00 AM. Mother is going to call me and let me know how he is when he comes out. Sorry I didn't write sooner but we have been so busy and I just wrote 2 letters & still owe some more
Pg2
We have our first game and our Junior play the 22nd of this month.
Is it ever nice out this last week. Have you heard from Belvin? I did he plans on marrying a woman with 2 boys.
Last Friday night we had a dance here at school a Royalty dance and I was candidate for Queen out of our homeroom. But the Seniors took it for King and Queen.
Pg 3
Gosh I'm tired I already wrote 2 letters this hour. So that will probably make yours short.
 Have you heard from Jerry?
Guess I'd better close almost time for classes to pass.
As Ever A Pen Pal,
Marilyn
P.S. Hope you can read this

2062 Morrish St.
Flint Michigan
July 27, 1949
Dear Betty,
Read your letter
yesterday and thought
I had better answer
before it slips my mind.
My but it's been hot
these last few days.
I've been so busy trying
to do all I wanted to do
during my vacation,
cleaning house and
getting ready for
school. I can hardly
wait, we start back
Pg 2
Sept 1 this is my last
year and most exciting.
Hate to see it go but I
suppose after I'm out I
can catch a man and
hook him for life.
I was looking at the
scenery in the picture it
looks like that sure is
beautiful country.
Bet you kids had fun
that day. I always like
to go some place with
just my guy and
another couple.
Pg 3
Seems you always have
fun. Sorry to hear about
all your bad luck. I
hope you get along ok
now. Everyone here is
feeling fine again.
Have you heard from
Belvin lately? I haven't
heard from him since
he was in Panama.
I plan on wring to him
this afternoon when I
finish this.

Pg 4
Tonight I;m going to get the
car and a bunch of us girls
are going to the drive in
Theater.
We always have fun during
the summer when we go
stag.
Guess I'll close
will write more next time.
As Ever Marilyn

New Meadows, Idaho
Box 225
Sept. 28, 53

Dear Marilyn,

Hi, How are you? Fine and in the best of health I do Hope. As for me I am doing fine.

It's been a very long time since I've heard from you. But I guess it was my own fault.

I guess I never did answer your last letter.

But I was always so damn busy. Taking care of mother.

She suffered for two years with a stroke. She pass away

Belvin Kroger
Jan. 6, 1945
Long Beach

Hello Betty Lou,

A happy new year to you, and am sure its not to late for the well wishes of the many months ahead.

I am sorry I keep you waiting so long but so sure was I that I would get to go home, but I like many had to stay here and it will be some time again before I will have a chance, I am now soon going to China a load of wheat and maybe gone for a few months but I shall come back and maybe by that time most of the boys will be home and the trains not so crowded it sure has been a mess out here of late. I worked Xmas and New Year but was just as well
Page 2   of as every where ones trys to go is crowded and one cant have any fun.

I see by the paper you have had some nasty weather up your way lots of snow and some cold weather to go with it, I have not seen any snow in so long I don't know what it looks like any more.

But maybe soon we will see some as we are going up to Portland from here to load, and there I have a kid Brother I have not seen for at least twenty years so I shall pay him a visit while there. And Betty Lou how is every

Thing with you there these days did you have a lovely Xmas and a grand happy new year I hope you did even though I could not be there and are you still working on your scrap book I wish

Page 3

You would send me one if you can.

I suppose your Brother in laws are out of the service by now and that should make every body happy.

And I hope that soon I can take of over the country again and see some of my friends for a change. May these lines find you at your best, tell all the folks hello

As ever

Your Friend Bill

Belvin O. Kroger

Ss James H Lane

c/o DE-L.A. Rama ss. Co.

Pier-A- Long Beach Calif

Belvin Kroger Pacific Ocean March 15,1945

Dear Friend Betty Lou,

You have called yourself a nervey little sister, and why have I not heard from you. It would please me very much to here from a girl with the fortitude and personality that you have there are not many girls that possess the quality that you have, and my only hope is that you do make good use off everything, you can really go places and be some body if you would like to.

Some of these days I am going to take a vacation, and would it surprise you if some day

Page 2

I would call on you for a little chat, it could happen. Today has been more or less a sober day for everyone we attended a funeral for one of our Navy gunners the first casualty on the ship he was buried on one of the Islands here in the Pacific with a lot of others some we know.

However everything in general is just fine we are getting a little low on things to eat not to much water as we have been out for quite some time now. And now how are you getting along in school and what do you want to be, what subject do

Page 3

you like the best.

And I would like very much to see that lake I'll bet I could have a swell time there, have they any places to dance

Hopeing these lines may find you at your best   As ever your
Friend Belvin

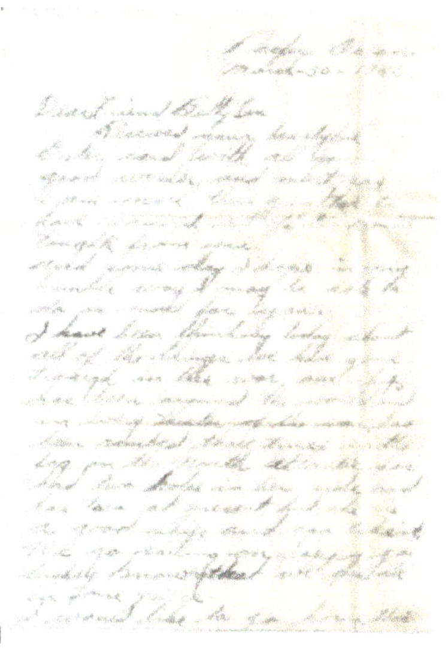

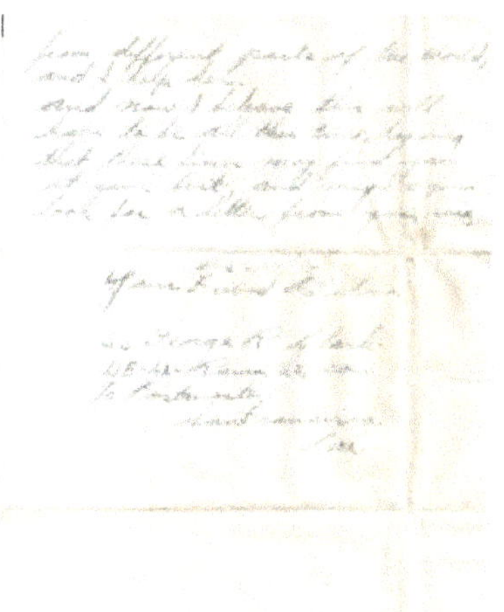

Bill Kroger
Pacific Ocean
March 30, 1945

Dearest Friend Betty Lou

Received your beautiful Ester card with all your good wishes, an must say I am more that grateful to have received all of these nice toughts from you. And some day I hope in my humble way I may be able to do as much for you. I have been thinking today about all of the things we have gone trough in the war, our ship has been around the world and in every theater of the war, has been rambed three times in the fog on the North Atlantic has had two holes in her side and has two at present, but she is a good ship and can take it. We go sailing on happy go lucky know that we are all in one piece. I would like to go home this

 Page 2

Time when I get back to the States, as I have not see my Mother since Dec. 1938 and that is a long time, she writes often at her age off 86 and has her good health, and has her work to do every day, she has been quite a girl in her day,

she sure has a lot of friends, every body thinks she is aces, and of course that don't make me feel bad.

Betty I get writers cramp when trying to keep up with the mail, I have this month written 76 letters, and received 90 so you see I am still not up to date but give me time and I will get there. And would I ever enjoy seeing one of your scrap books, I have one of my own and it has many things of interest in it, and pictures that I have been able to get in different ports, and I have a neice that has a hobby off collecting pictures
page 3

From different parts of the World, and I help her. And now I beleave this will have to be all this time, hopeing that these lines may find you at your best, and may I again look for a letter from you, sure

As ever
Your Friend Belvin   SS
George R. Clark
DE-4A-Rama S.S. CO.
c/o Postmaster
San Francisco, Cal.

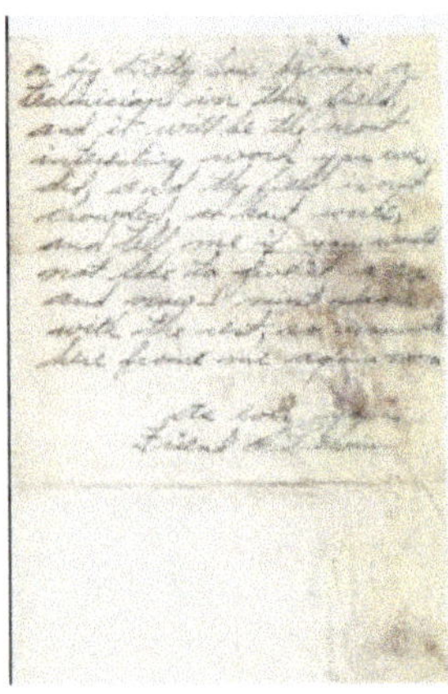

Belvin Kroger
May 1, 1945
San Francisco
Calif

Dear Friend Betty Lou,

Arrived this morning 3:40 AM May 1, 1945 A.D., and your most welcome letter awaited me upon arrival here. It sure feels grand to be back and see lights at night, and have no fear that some high above may drop an egg any minute and blow you to bits.

Yes I know you are a little girl, but I also know you have at your age done big things, so age don't have to much bearing on anyone I think your are grand.

Page 2

You like others, I know hate school and would rather do something else, but look Betty Lou try and love to go to school, study hard and always remember no mater how old you get, there is always more to learn about the world that we live in today.

The war to most people as I see it today, is quite some difference than it should be, Victory will not be won it Europe on the far East, but here in San Francisco

At the Peace Conference, that is the most important history of the day. Can this conference accomplish what it set out to do, then in the future we may (pg.3) look forward to progress and happiness, if not then we will have something to worry about, as in the past and you say you want to be a power house operator and I believe you should be what you want to be, however that will be taking the easy way out and we all ready have to many that think the same as you.

Now the work you have been doing for the boys over seas, is something that one don't see to much off, and a lot of that kind of work is so badly needed in times of peace. And why cant our little

Page 4

or big Betty Lou become a technician in the field, and it will be the most interesting work you ever did, and the field is not crowded, at least write and tell me if you would not like to give it a try and now I must share with the rest, so you will here from me again soon.

As Ever your

Friend Belvin

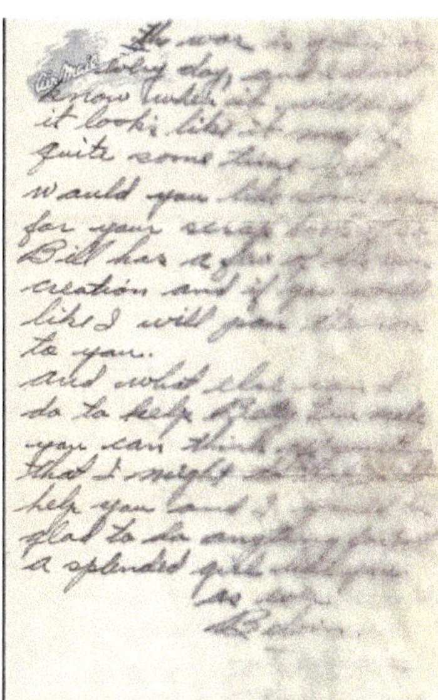

Belvin Kroger
Kanulua, Kawaii
June 10, 1945

Hello Betty Lou

Today Bill has a agains and I have had so many. That really I don't need to have any more but they seem to creep up on one so often.

And it looked like all the native girls were dressed for my birthday I never did see so many flowers as I see today it was a sight and Fragrance beyond anything that I have witnessed in my day.

Had quite a day I did see so much beautie today birds from all parts of the world one can see here

page 2

Is just the grandest place I have ever see, they have everything to make people happy a lovely beach play grounds of all kinds and then I went to a show and it was very good so the some total I would say Bill had a lovely day.

However they tell me it is a great deal better in pease time, just to many people here now every place one goes it is crowded. And I like lots of room and you did ask for a snap shot and will send you one just as soon as I can get some more all out at present.

Page 3

The war is going on every day and I don't know when it will end. It looks like it may be quite some time yet.

Would you like some poems for your scrap book if so Bill has a few of his own creation and if you would like I will pass them on to you.

And what else can I do to help Betty Lou mabe you can think off something that I might do that would help you and I would be glad to do anything for just a splendid girl like you.

As Ever

Belvin

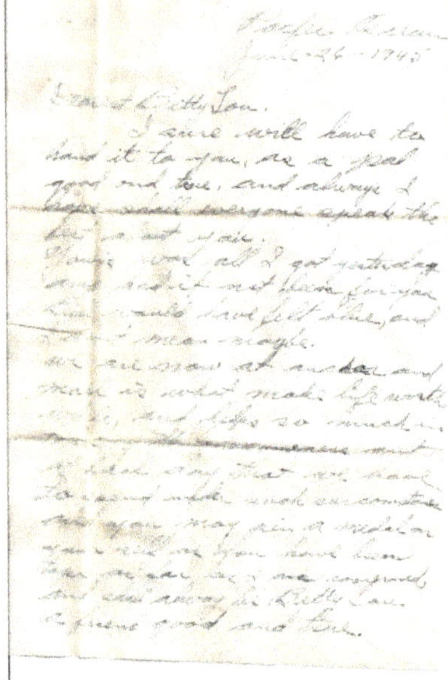

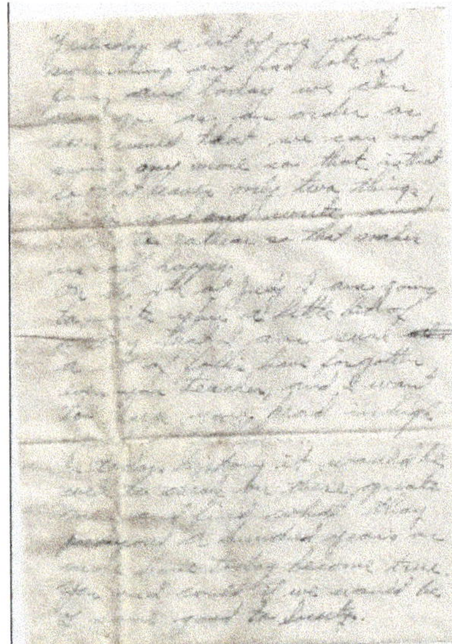

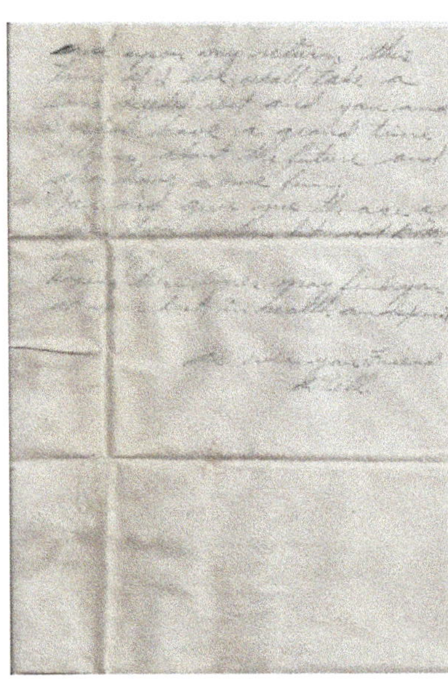

Bill Kroger
Pacific Ocean
June 26, 1945

Dearest Betty Lou,

I sure would have to hand it to you, as a pal and true, and always I hope shall everyone speak the best about you.

Yours was all I got yesterday and had it not been for you Bill would have felt blue, and I don't mean maybe.

We are now at anchor and mail is what make life worthwhile, and helps so much in takes the lonesomeness out of each day that we have to spend under such surcomstances and you may pin a medal on your self as you have been tops as far as I am concerded and shall always be Betty Lou a friend good and true.

Page 2

Yesterday a lot of us went swimming and had lots of fun and today we can not go as an order has been issued that we can not swim any more so that is that. So that leaves only two things, to go read and write and I like to eathear or (eat hear) so that makes us all happy.

On the 4th of July I am going to write you a little bit of history that I am sure a lot of folks have forgotten even your teacher, and I want to keep your head in high speed at all times.

In todays history it would be swell to check on these greats men and find what thay predisposed a hundred year's or more have today become true. You and I could if we would be of some good to Society.

Page 3

And upon my return this time if I live, shall take a long needed rest and you and I shall have a grand time talking about the future and also have some fun.

You did give me the age of your two brothers but not Betty Lou why?

Hope these lines may find you at your best, in health and spirit.

As ever your friend

Bill

Bill Kroger
Pacific Ocean
July 21, 1945

Hello Betty

Received your card and letter today and just can say a word to express my appreciation, however it did find me feeling tops and waiting for the mail as we have not received any for so long. And I am not afraid of cougars or any other animal in fact, and I like to hunt and fish go exploring and what not, I do wish I could have been there with you.

Now the heat has been extreme out here of late, and I have been out cold once just could not take it I guise, but I did drink some ice water at the time and it did not take long after that before Bill was out cold, and I will do better next time.

The mail has been very slow up to date but hope it get better however we can not expect to

Much at present, there are many others like myself.

Its possible that we shall not have any leave until we get back to the states so our letters mean so much to us at present, that to here from you after would be highly appreciated.

The boys to date have been splendid fellows they have an art of doing things when things get dull thay do a lot of the things you do, and every once in a while a picture cut out of a magazine and write a note about some one in the crew and we all get a big kick out of it.

And also as things stand now on my way East when I get back I hope to see you I wont be able to stay long but will do my best to make my stay a plesent one.

So lets cross our fingers and hope for the future, that everything shall go well, so that I may see you soon.

As ever

Bill

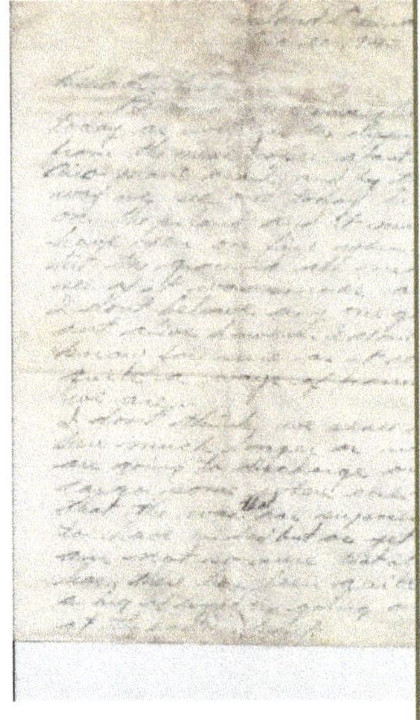

Bill Kroger
Island Okinawa
Aug. 20, 1945

Hello Betty Lou,

Received your lovely letter today as well as the clips from the news paper about the Airo plane crash, and by the way we see one today here on the Island and it must have been on fire when it hit the ground all one could see of it was smoke and I don't beleave any one got out alive however I don't know for sure as it was quite a ways of from where we are.

I don't think we shall be here much longer as we are going to discharge our cargo some where else now that the war that has supposed to have ended but as yet I am not so sure that it has, there has been quite a big of fighting going on at the eastern front.

Page 2

Up till just a few days ago as well as air raid alarms here two and three a night but the last few days have been quite. Where we go from here I don't know but will be on our way soon I hope we have been here to long as it is. And now it looks very much like Bill will see New Meadows as well as Betty Lou be for many months road by would you like to see Bill?

However I am going to spend some time in the West before going back east and maybe I will find a place in the mean time that I would like to make my home, and maybe I can find a girl that wants a home too wouldn't that be just grand. I think some thing like that is what Bill really wants.

Page 3

First I must find a girl that likes to travel and see things because my work will take me to all parts of the World I hope, I do have a lot of places that I want to see and I don't like to go alone I like company.

Do you suppose I will find a girl that would like to go and see beautiful thing to see what the rest of the world has and how thay live. One that would like to see every State in the good Old U.S.A. and to help plan and build for the future, one who would enjoy doing things that would make others happy.

I you should know of a girl of this type let me know I want to meet her. May these lines find you at your best as well as the rest of the folks out your way.

As ever

Your Bill

Belvin Kroger
Jan. 16, 1946
Long Beach

Dear Betty Lou

Received your welcome letter today and was glad to here from you and that all is well out your way. Having had the flu an many have had in these last months was not surprising, however by now the many cases have been taken care of and all is well on that front. Now we have many problems comfronting us to day housing being one on the list and I think it a shame to have let this housing program go un-checked as has been the case today, it will take years at the rate we are going and in the mean time our G.I. boys go without a place to

Page 2

Live, the cost is way out of reach for the average family. No one that works can pay ten thousand for a home or eighty dollars a month for rent as that seems to be what thay ask for a fairly deasent place.

Now Betty Lou this housing Problem may not seem like a lot to you, but may I now point out just how important it really is, its important enough to make or brake and nation, so now it is a job for all the people to put some push behind housing and I mean every body.

Jobs for our boys seem to be lagging as well as a raise in pay and the cost of living going up and soon if some thing isent done about it we will find our selves in a mess,

Page 3

The President seems to be pushing all he can, but Congress and Senate seem to be stalling on so many things that could have been settled now had thay done some thing about it before Xmas.

Now our orders have been changed and we are going to Toropilla, Chile and from there to France so by the time we get back it will be Spring or Summer I hope then I hope I can take a little vacation and maybe see our Betty Lou.

As ever

Your Friend Belvin

sS.S. James H. Lane
c/o U.S. Causul
Toropilla, Chile.

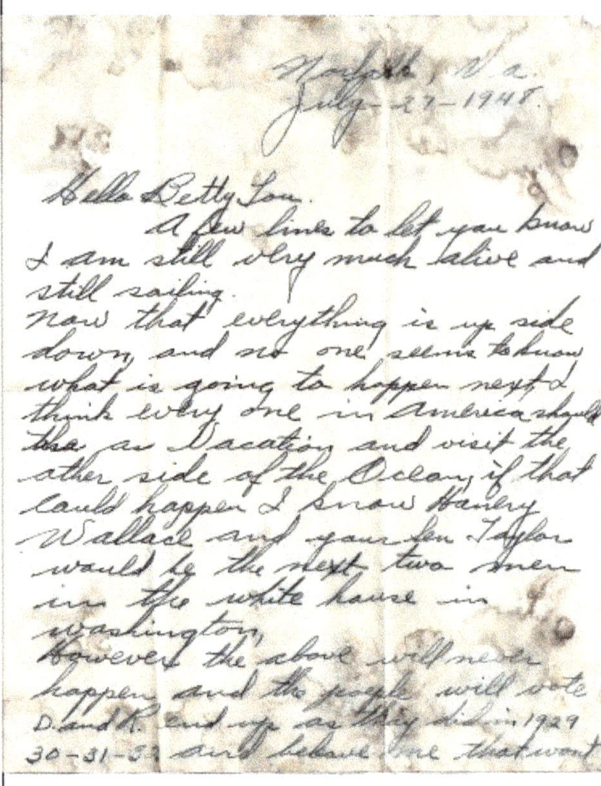

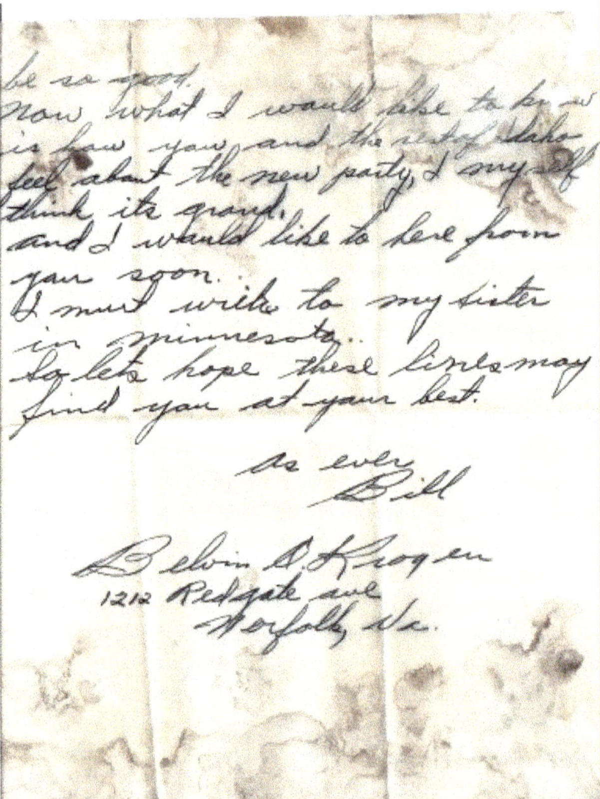

Bill Kroger
Norfolk, Va.
July 27, 1948

Hello Betty Lou
A few lines to let you know I am still very much a live and still sailing.
Now that everything is up side down, and no one seems to know what is going to happen next, I think every one in America should take as vacation and visit the other side of the Ocean, if that could happen I know Hanery Wallace and your Sen Taylor would be the next two men in the white house in Washington, However the above will never happen and the people will vote D. and R. end up as they did in 1929 30-31-32 and beleave me that wont
Page 2
 be so good
Now what I would like to know is how you and the rest of Idaho feel about the new party, I myself think its grand,
and I would like to here from you soon.
I must write to my sister in Minnesota.
So lets hope these lines may find you at your best.
As ever
Bill
Belvin O. Kroger
1212 Redgate Ave
Norfolk, Va.

Bill Kroger

Mobile, Ala. March 1, 1947
Pg.1
Hello Betty Lou,
I received your letter plus your picture and sure was happy you look wonderful and would not worry about the two shades is where your beauty lies.
I also received a picture and letter from Marilyn quite a girl it has been some time since I saw her last, but if some thing unforeseen does not show up I hope to see her this summer and also Alice another nice that lives at West Branch, Michigan, and maybe we shall see Betty Lou and some more of the U.S.A. However it sure don't look good for Bill, every day I
Pg.2
Call New Orleans and they want me to hurry back, and when I do I suppose they have something for me to do. I know it is needed so badly now, I did so much look forward to world peace I am sure we can have if we only knew more about the world at large.
I just got back from Pelermo, Sicley and it just about made me sick to think about the conditions there, very few boys and girls get to go to school more than two years, and unless that condition changes not much can be hoped for as far as Italy is concerned. Many as yet believe as they did before the war and when I say many I mean just that and back home things don't look a bit good, by June 30th all O.P.A. Regulations shall not be any more, and then we

Bill Kroger

Mobile, Ala. March 1, 1947

Continued

Pg 3
Will headed back to 1932 and
then we can do it all over again
maybe
So here we are Betty Lou going
down hill when we should be
going up, and the ones that
make
These reports could do a great
deal but don't.

All one reds about today is the
purge on communisum and surly
there are more important things
to take care of than these Reds,
they will git along all right for
sure.

I will cut short now I have more
letters to write.

And may these lines find you
Dad and mother Brother and
Sisters at your Best

As ever

Bill

415 Beinville St

New Orleans, La

Many years later Betty would marry Floyd Eugene Hunt and my Father.

Floyd served in WWII in seven campaigns. He fought off the coast of Africa and also in Sicily.

This photo was taken Sept. 16, 1943 in Sicily with other military buddies.

He cut the post card to fit in a collage so all I have is one other name, place, and date.

The only name is Harvey Kreiter

Floyd is on the top right, age 20.

Sgt. Charles H. Wolverton of the U.S. 37th Division. Prepares to throw a hand grenade at a Japanese Pill Box on Bougainville, Solomen Island.

BITING his tongue, Sgt. Charles H. Wolverton of the U. S. 37th division, prepares to throw a hand grenade at a Jap pillbox on Bougainville, Solomen islands. A moment later, he scored a perfect hit on the target, blowing it apart. Signal corps photo. (International.)

Betty Lou (Ross) Hunt

Betty Lou (Ross) Hunt, 70, of Boise, died Sunday, May 16 in a Boise hospital.

A private family memorial will be held at a later date in New Meadows, Idaho.

Betty was born on April 1, 1934 in Middleton, Idaho to Frank and Alma (Ward) Ross. She was the youngest girl of 8 children. Her father worked for J.I. Morgan logging. They moved around living in Old Cabarton, Old McGreggor and finally settling in New Meadows. Betty helped with the war effort by watching for and reporting planes coming in from Canada. She was also commended by the Secretary of War for collecting and sending scrap books and letters to soldiers.

Betty met and married Floyd Hunt. They had a daughter, Linda. Betty and Linda later moved to New Meadows. Betty worked for the Continental Telephone Company until 1964. Betty and Linda then moved to Boise into the Fiesta Trailer Park where Betty lived until her death. She worked for Nasua, Conchemco for 13 years then Hewlett Packard for 15 years until ill health forced her to retire. Betty loved the mountains, her cabin, her family, fishing, hunting, playing cards and playing pool.

She is survived by her daughter and son-in-law Linda and David Roberts of Meridian; sister and brother-in-law Dorothy and Warren Loonies of New Meadows; brother and sister-in-law John and Margaret Ross of Puyallup, Wash.; sister-in-law Vineta Ross of New Meadows; grandson Timothy Roberts, the light of her life; and numerous nieces and nephews. Special fishing buddies ex-sister-in-law Esther Fisher of Mountain Home, extended family Vern Bohn, Patty Dobson, Ben Lema.

Betty was preceded in death by her parents Frank and Alma, infant daughter Debra Ann, brothers Frank Jr, Bill Ross, Jack (Ed) Ross, Fred Ross, and sister Camiliea (Celie) Conner.

Mom's struggle finally ended courageously with family by her side. I love you Honey.

Mom was laid to rest here in New Meadows, Idaho where she grew up.

www.ingramcontent.com/pod-product-compliance
Lightning Source LLC
Chambersburg PA
CBHW041148300726
48978CB00017B/1423